The Ugly Dino Hatchling

by Stephanie Peters

MG (4-8)
ATOS 2.3
0.5 pts
Fiction

189571 EN

P9-CAM-487

FAR OUT
FABLES

STONE ARCH BOOKS
a capstone imprint

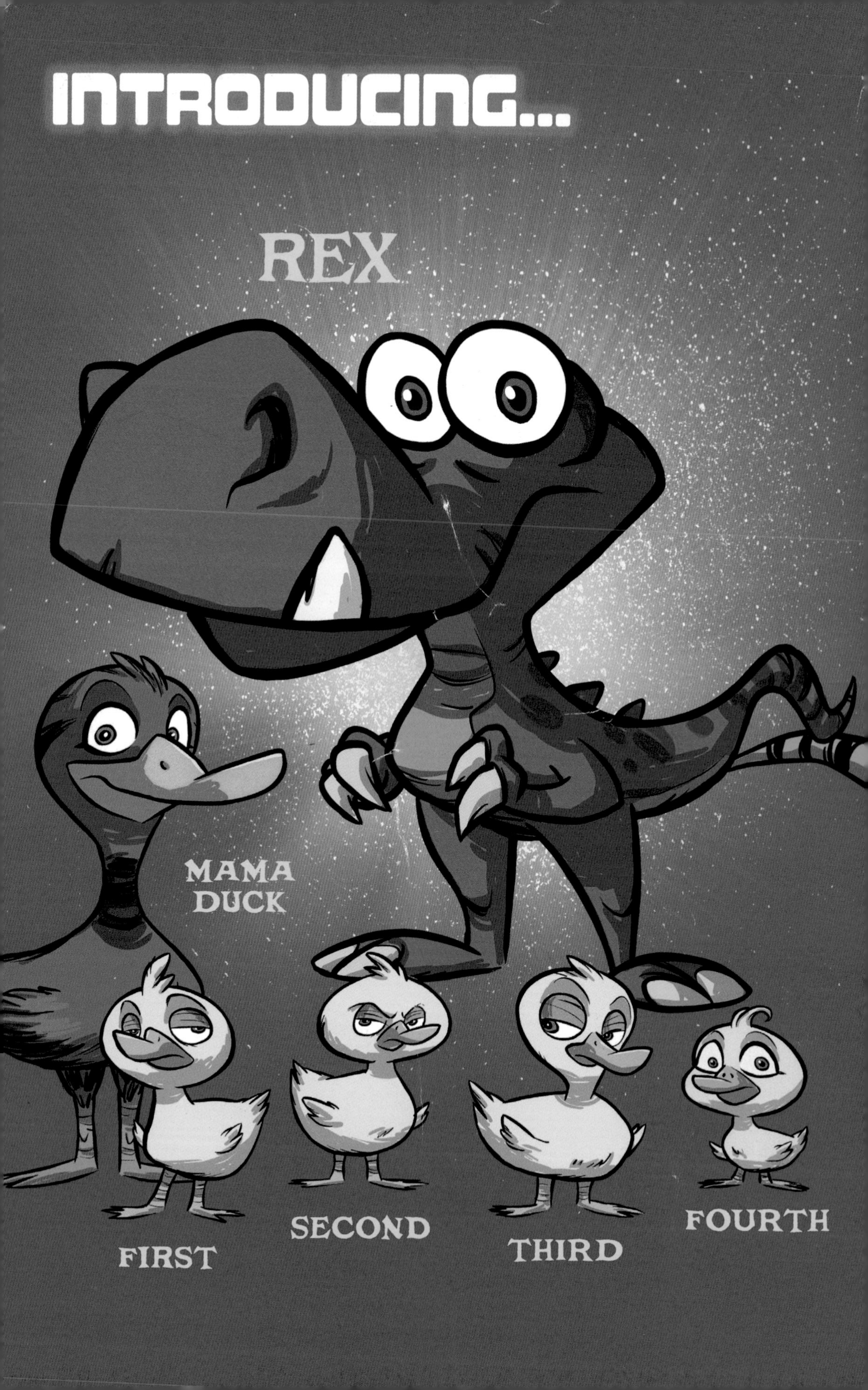
INTRODUCING...
REX
MAMA DUCK
FIRST
SECOND
THIRD
FOURTH

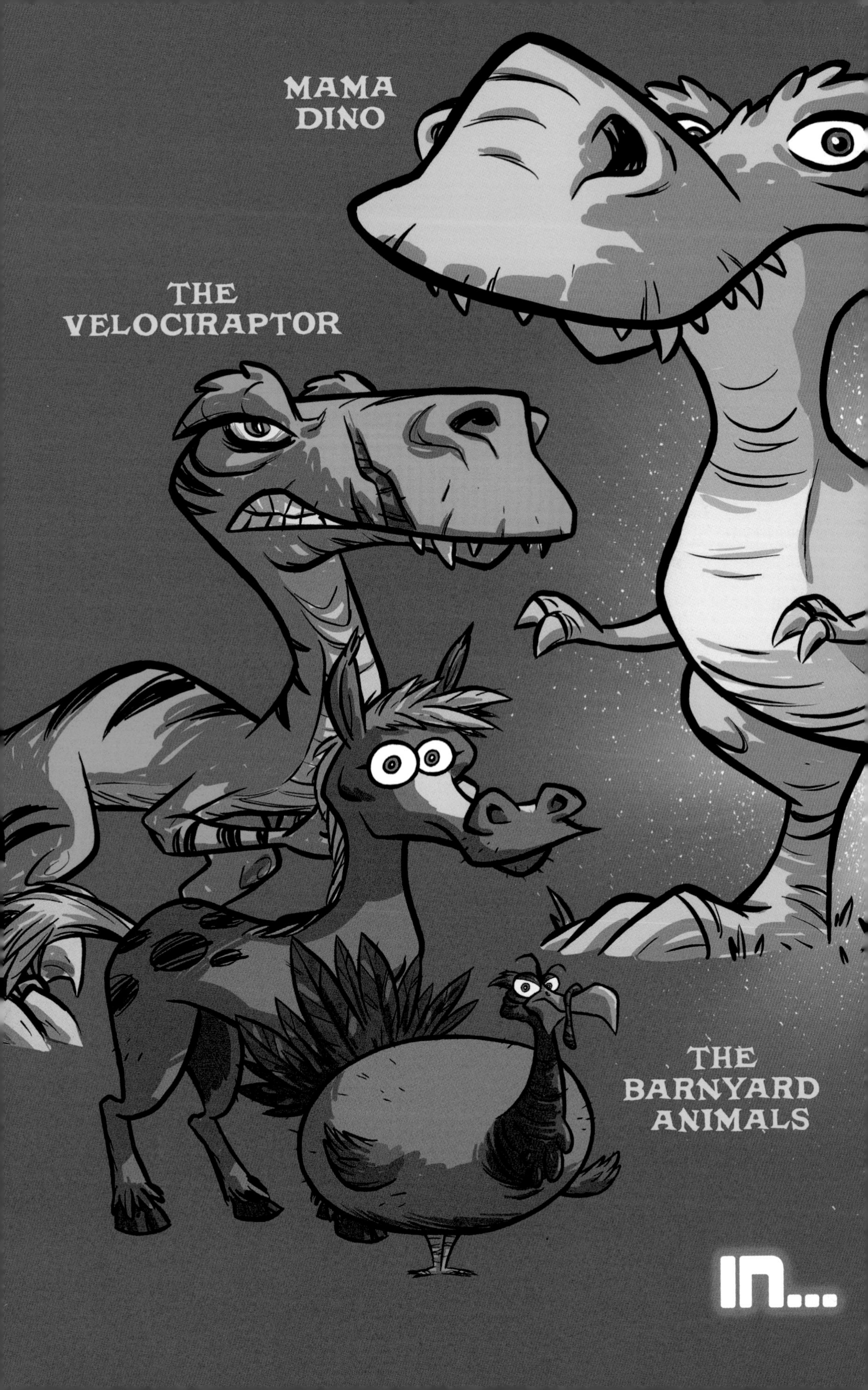
MAMA DINO
THE VELOCIRAPTOR
THE BARNYARD ANIMALS
IN...

Far Out Fables is published by
Stone Arch Books
A Capstone Imprint
1710 Roe Crest Drive
North Mankato, Minnesota 56003
www.mycapstone.com

Copyright © 2018 by Stone Arch
Books. All rights reserved. No part of
this publication may be reproduced
in whole or in part, or stored in a
retrieval system, or transmitted in
any form or by any means, electronic,
mechanical, photocopying, recording,
or otherwise, without written
permission of the publisher.

Cataloging-in-Publication Data is
available at the Library of Congress
website.
ISBN 978-1-4965-5419-2 (hardcover)
ISBN 978-1-4965-5423-9 (paperback)
ISBN 978-1-4965-5427-7 (eBook PDF)

Summary: A dino egg has tumbled
through a time portal and into a duck's
nest. But it's obvious the hatchling Rex
doesn't fit in. He can't swim, he can't
quack, and he looks REALLY different.
What's worse, something else —
something dangerous — is about to
travel through the portal. Will Rex
be able save his friends and find out
where he truly belongs?

Designed by Hilary Wacholz
Edited by Abby Huff
Lettered by Jaymes Reed

Printed in the USA.
010371F17

FAR OUT FABLES

THE UGLY DINO HATCHLING

A GRAPHIC NOVEL

BY STEPHANIE PETERS

ILLUSTRATED BY OTIS FRAMPTON

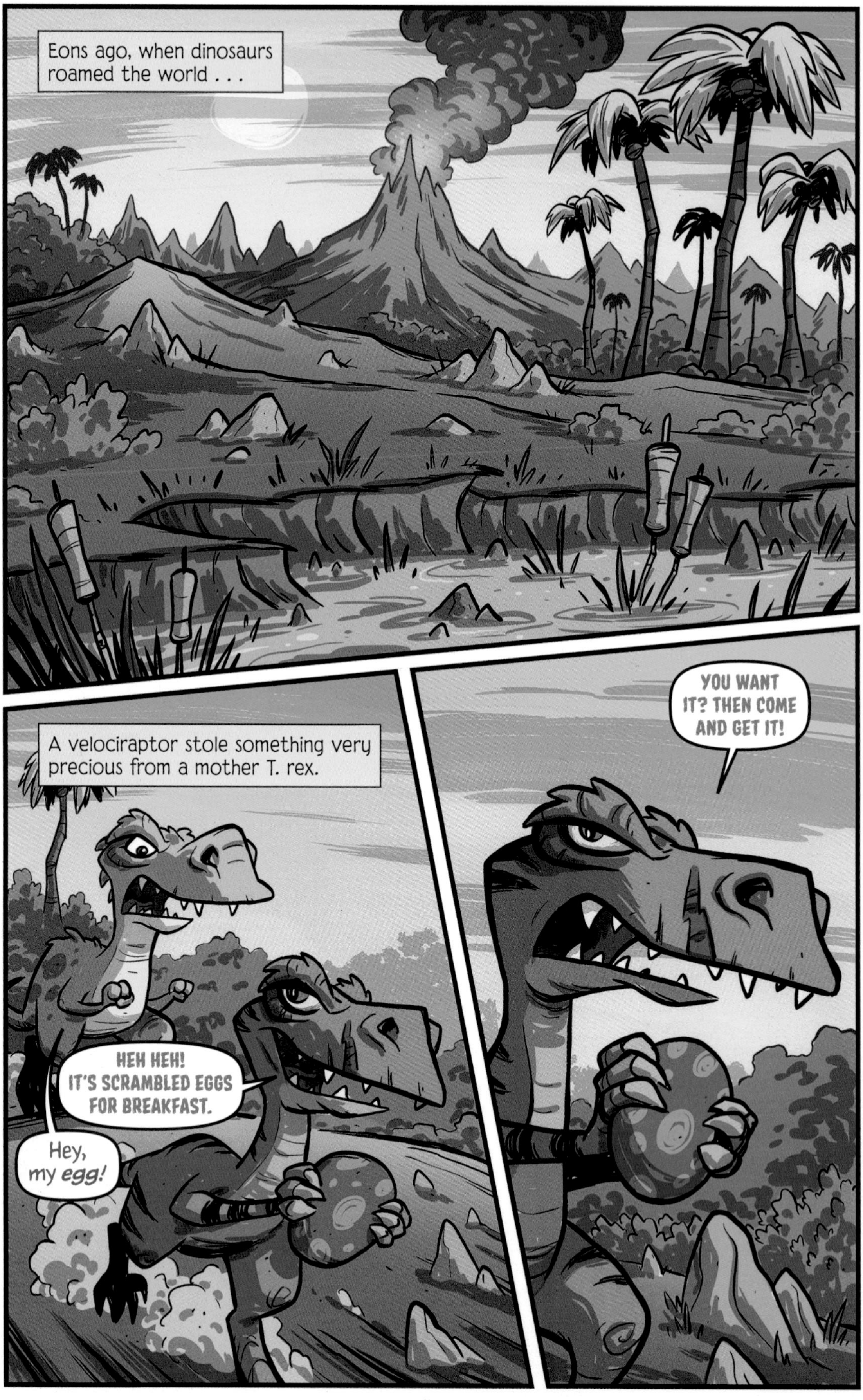
Eons ago, when dinosaurs roamed the world . . .
A velociraptor stole something very precious from a mother T. rex.
HEH HEH! IT'S SCRAMBLED EGGS FOR BREAKFAST.
Hey, my *egg!*
YOU WANT IT? THEN COME AND GET IT!

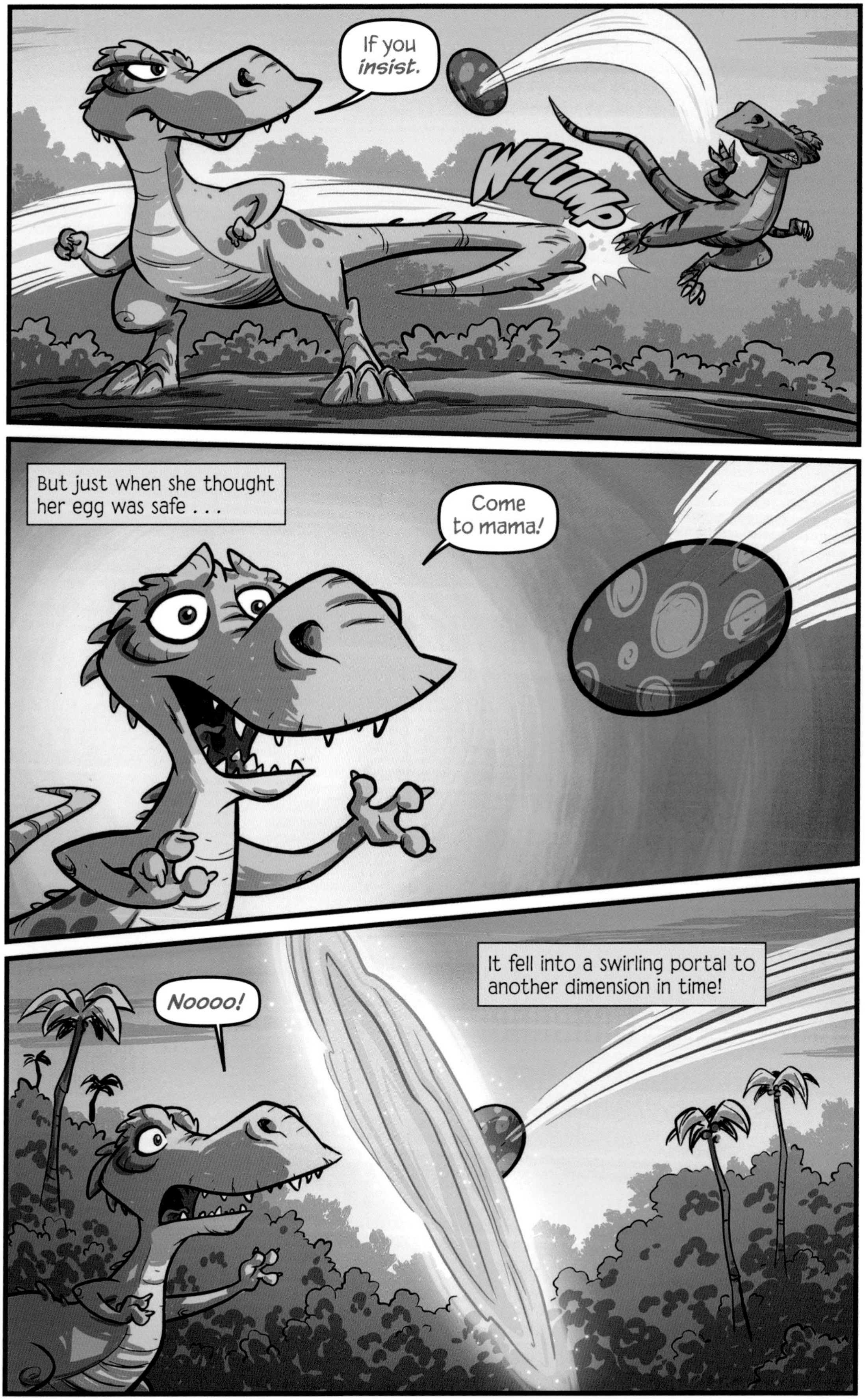

If you *insist.*
WHUMP
But just when she thought her egg was safe . . .
Come to mama!
It fell into a swirling portal to another dimension in time!
Noooo!

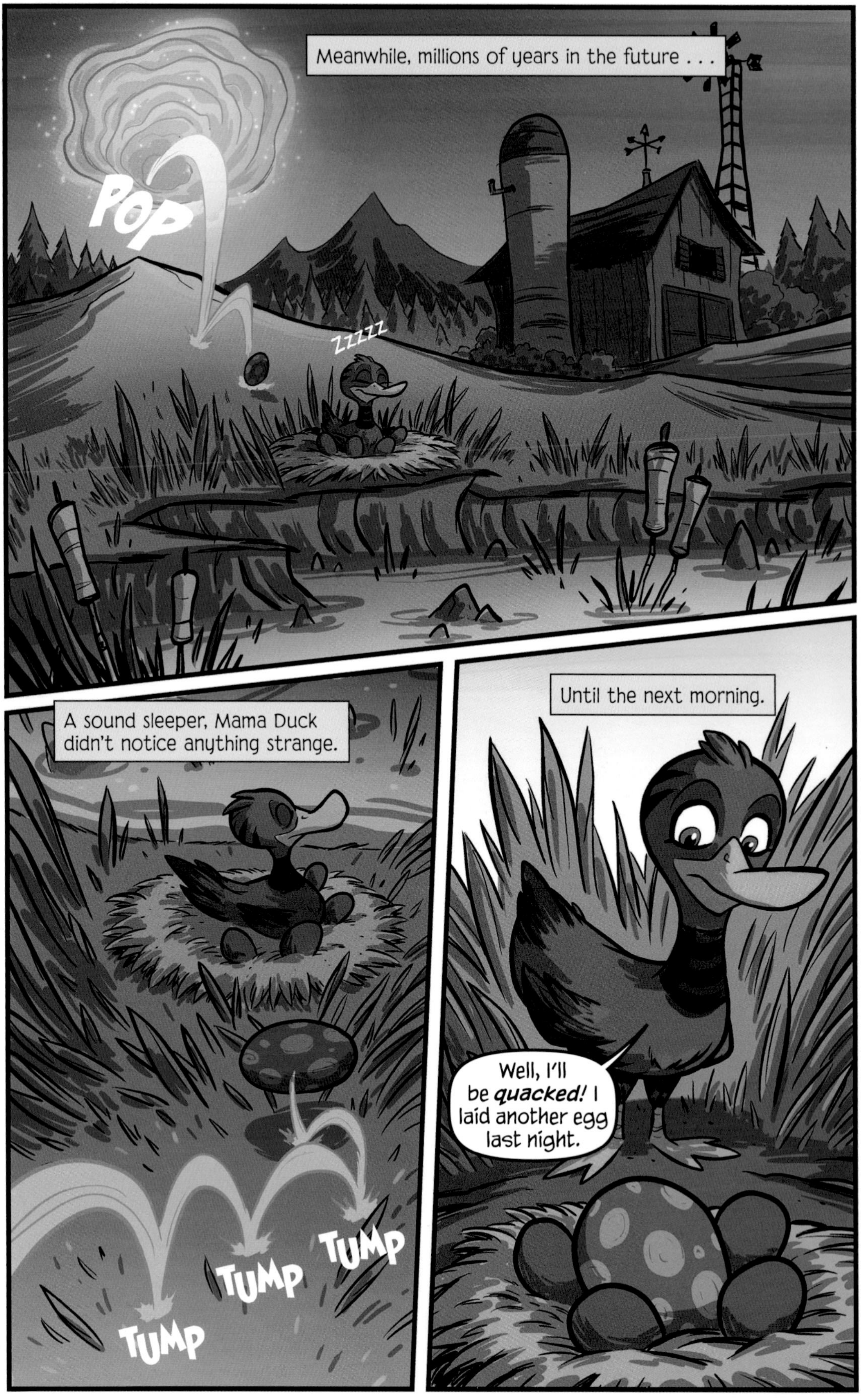
Meanwhile, millions of years in the future . . .
POP
ZZZZZ
A sound sleeper, Mama Duck didn't notice anything strange.
TUMP
TUMP
TUMP
Until the next morning.
Well, I'll be *quacked!* I laid another egg last night.

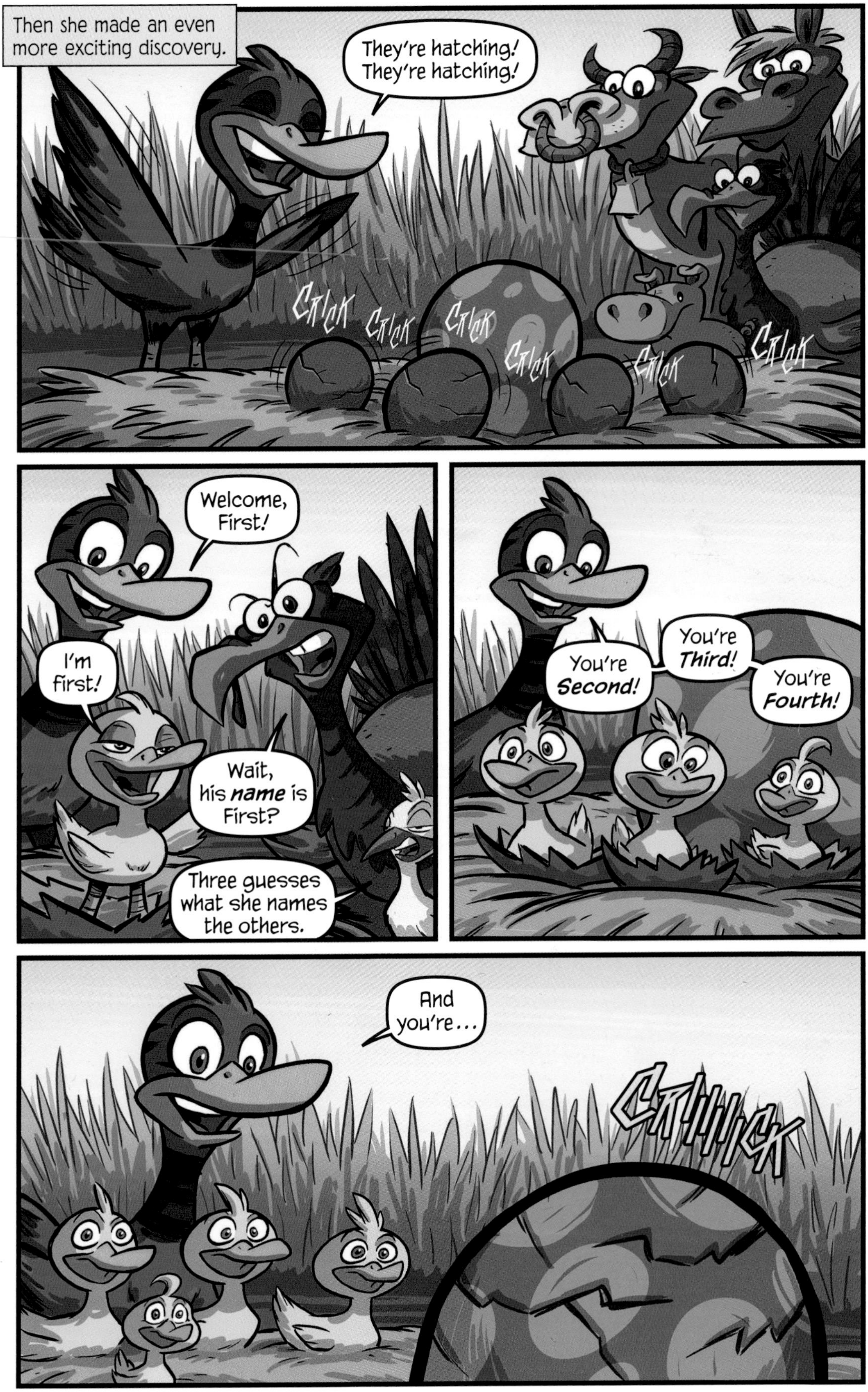

Then she made an even more exciting discovery.
They're hatching! They're hatching!
CRICK
CRICK
CRICK
CRICK
CRICK
CRICK
Welcome, First!
I'm first!
Wait, his **name** is First?
Three guesses what she names the others.
You're **Second!**
You're **Third!**
You're **Fourth!**
And you're...
CRIIIICK

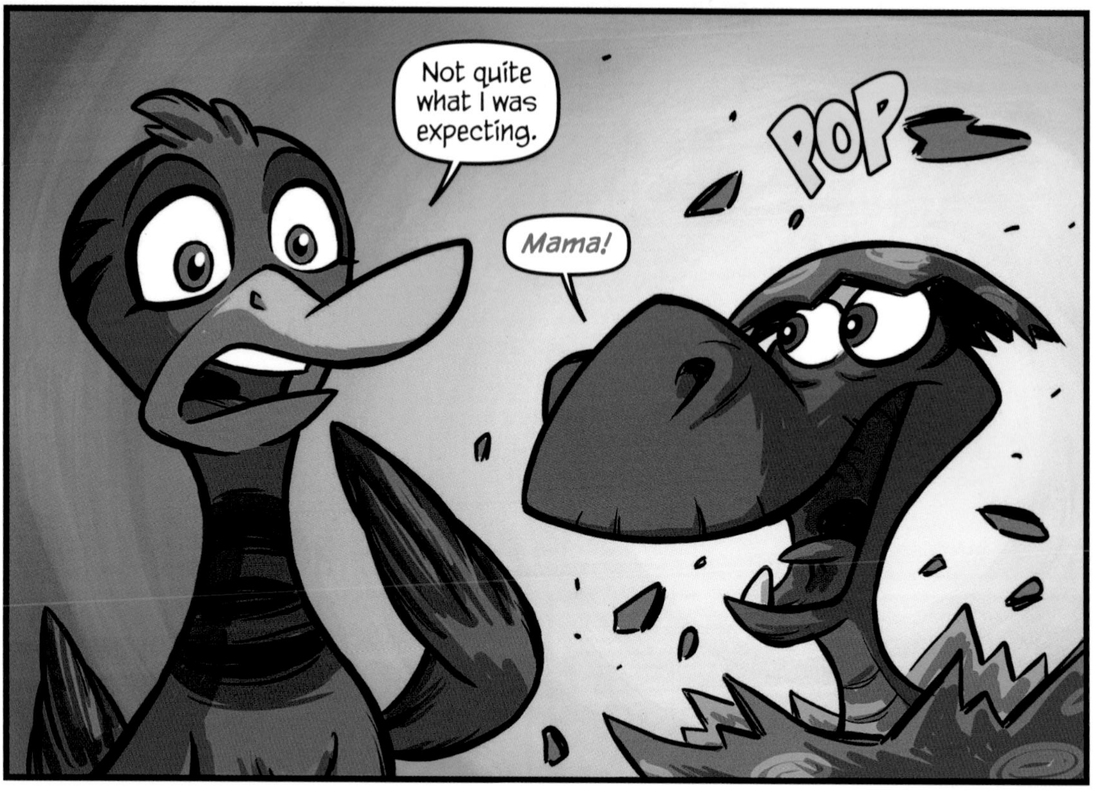
Not quite what I was expecting.
POP
Mama!

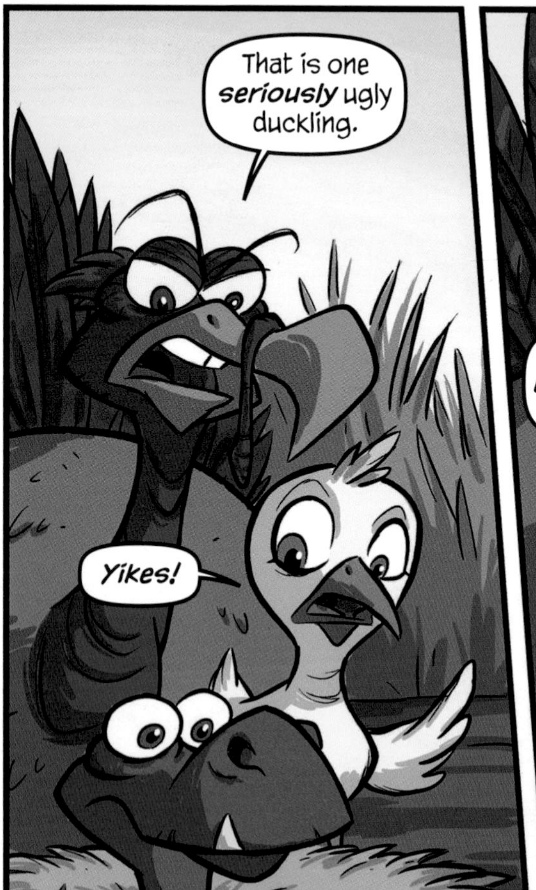
That is one *seriously* ugly duckling.
Yikes!

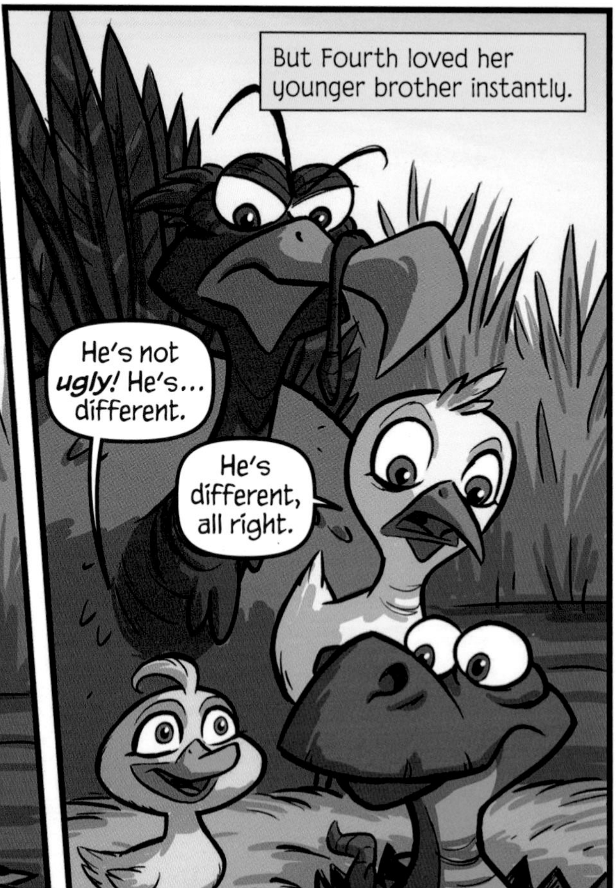
But Fourth loved her younger brother instantly.
He's not *ugly!* He's... different.
He's different, all right.

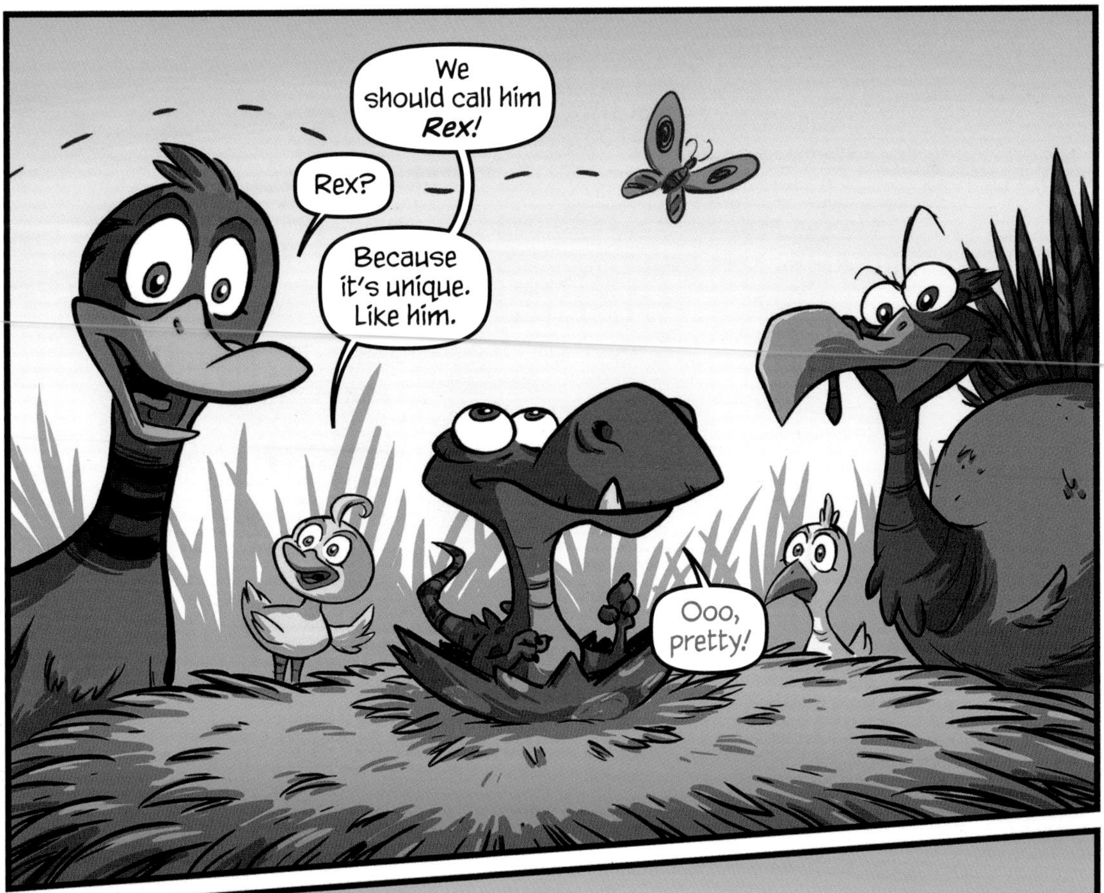
We should call him *Rex!*
Rex?
Because it's unique. Like him.
Ooo, pretty!

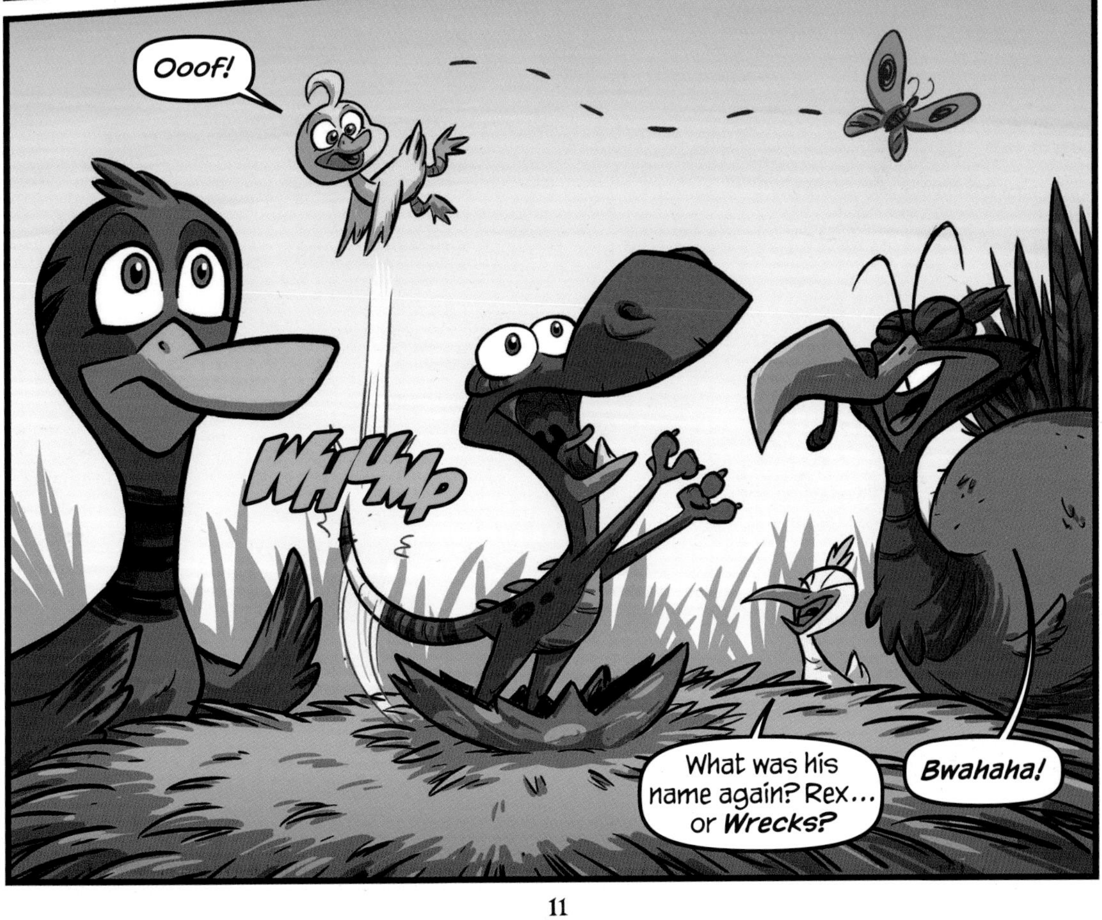
Ooof!
WHUMP
What was his name again? Rex... or *Wrecks?*
Bwahaha!

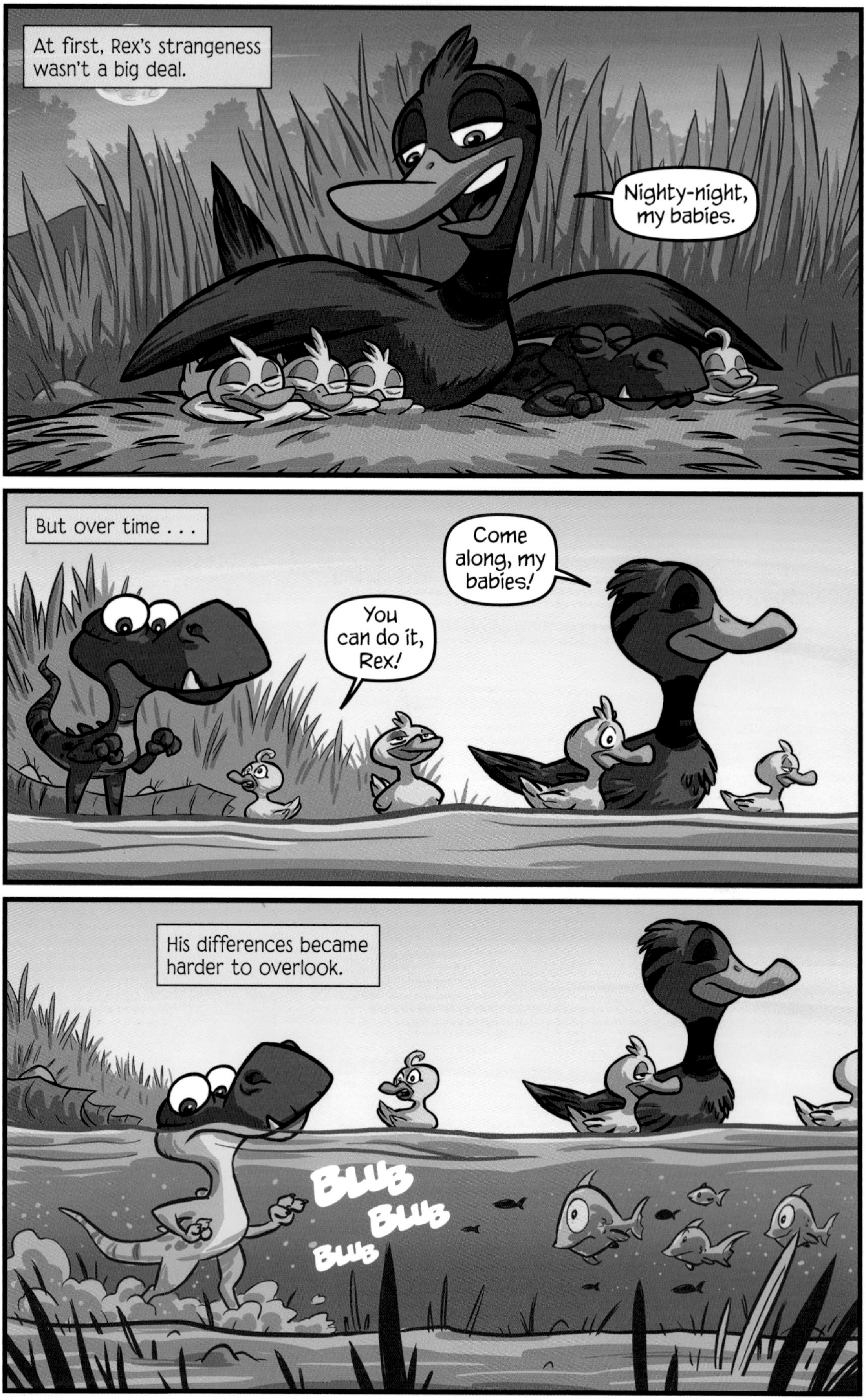
At first, Rex's strangeness wasn't a big deal.
Nighty-night, my babies.
But over time . . .
Come along, my babies!
You can do it, Rex!
His differences became harder to overlook.
BLUB
BLUB
BLUB

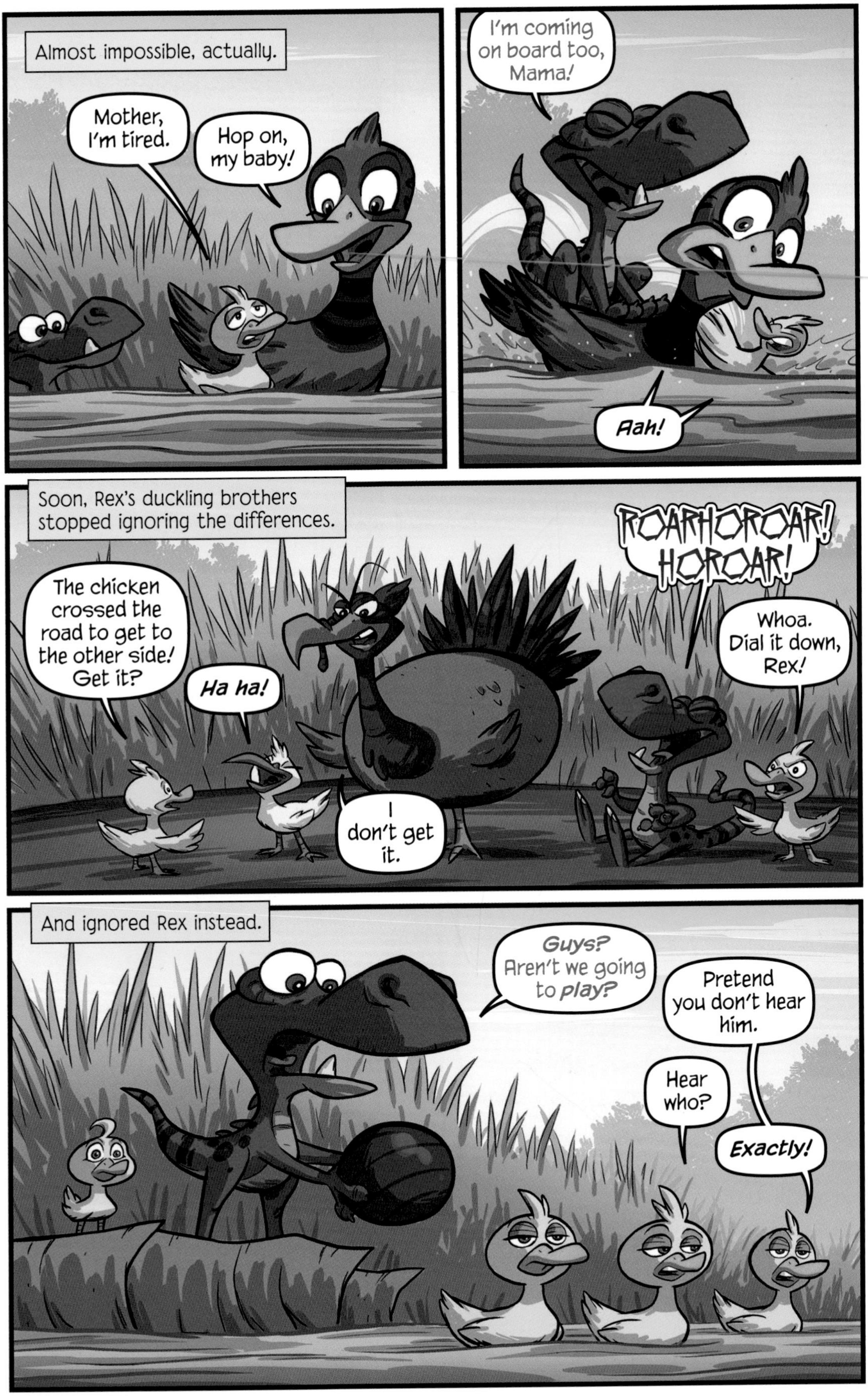
Almost impossible, actually.
Mother, I'm tired.
Hop on, my baby!
I'm coming on board too, Mama!
Aah!
Soon, Rex's duckling brothers stopped ignoring the differences.
The chicken crossed the road to get to the other side! Get it?
Ha ha!
I don't get it.
ROARHOROAR! HOROAR!
Whoa. Dial it down, Rex!
And ignored Rex instead.
Guys? Aren't we going to play?
Pretend you don't hear him.
Hear who?
Exactly!

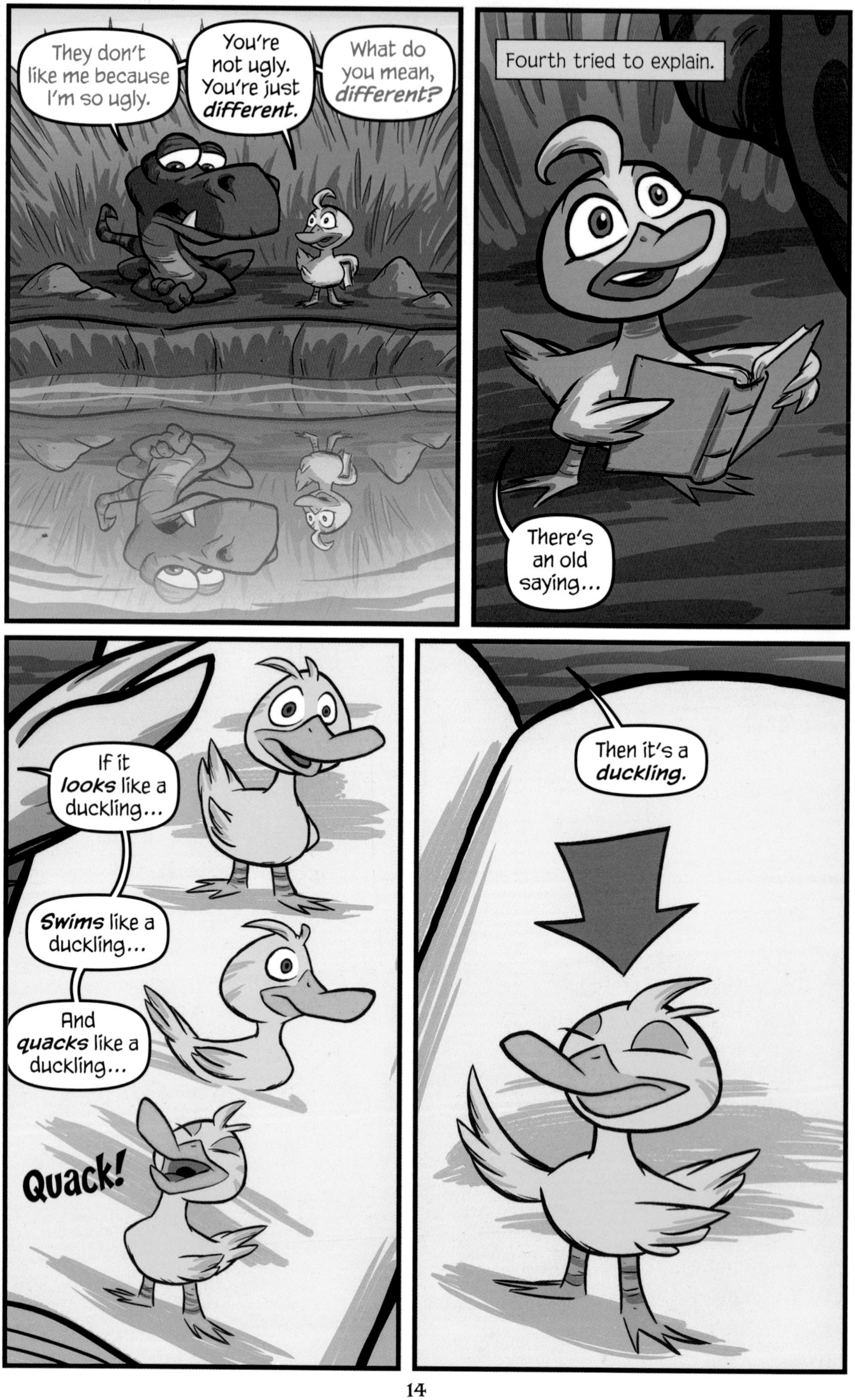
They don't like me because I'm so ugly.
You're not ugly. You're just **different**.
What do you mean, **different?**
Fourth tried to explain.
There's an old saying...
If it **looks** like a duckling...
Swims like a duckling...
And **quacks** like a duckling...
Quack!
Then it's a **duckling**.

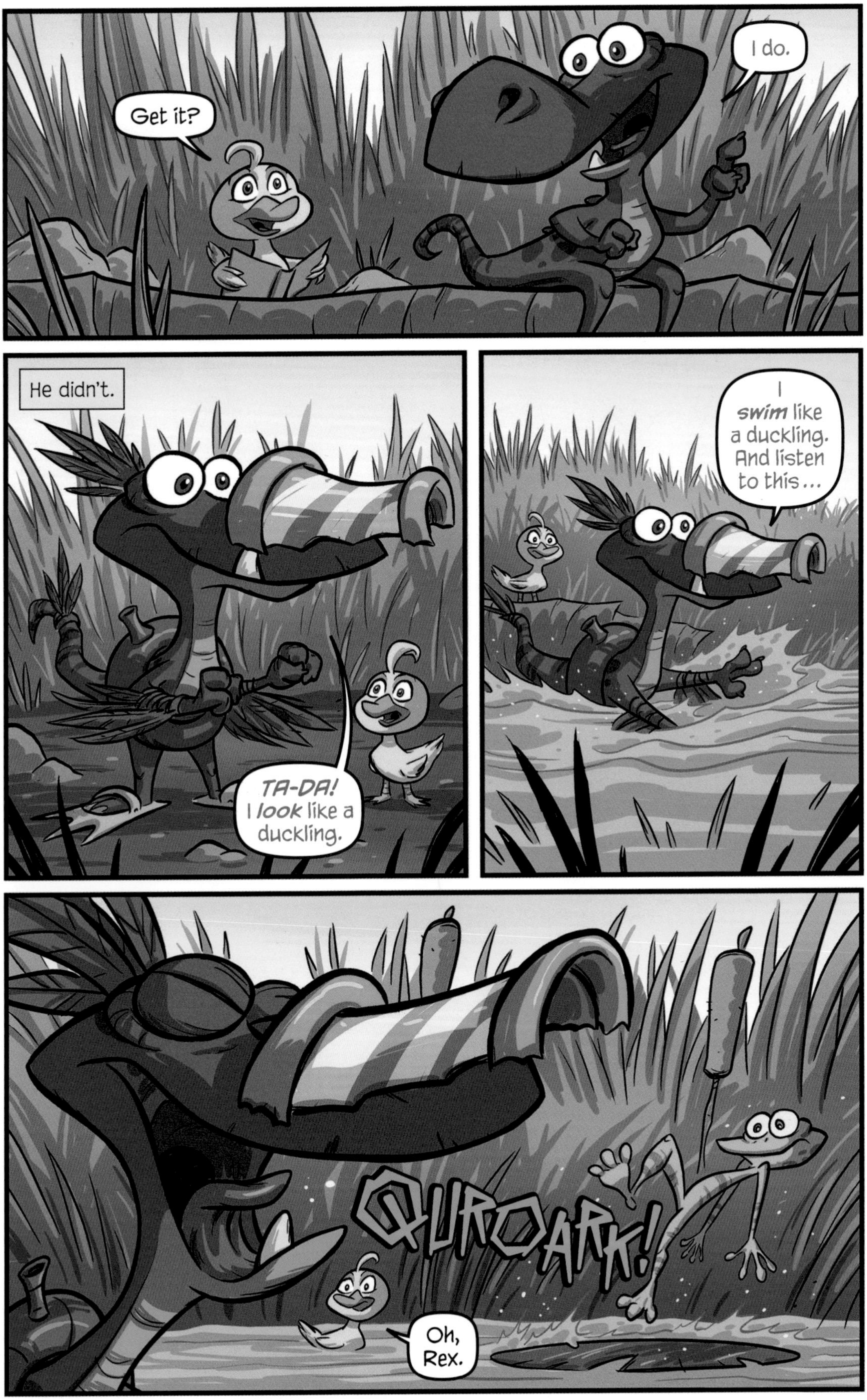
Get it?
I do.
He didn't.
TA-DA! I *look* like a duckling.
I *swim* like a duckling. And listen to this...
QUROARK!
Oh, Rex.

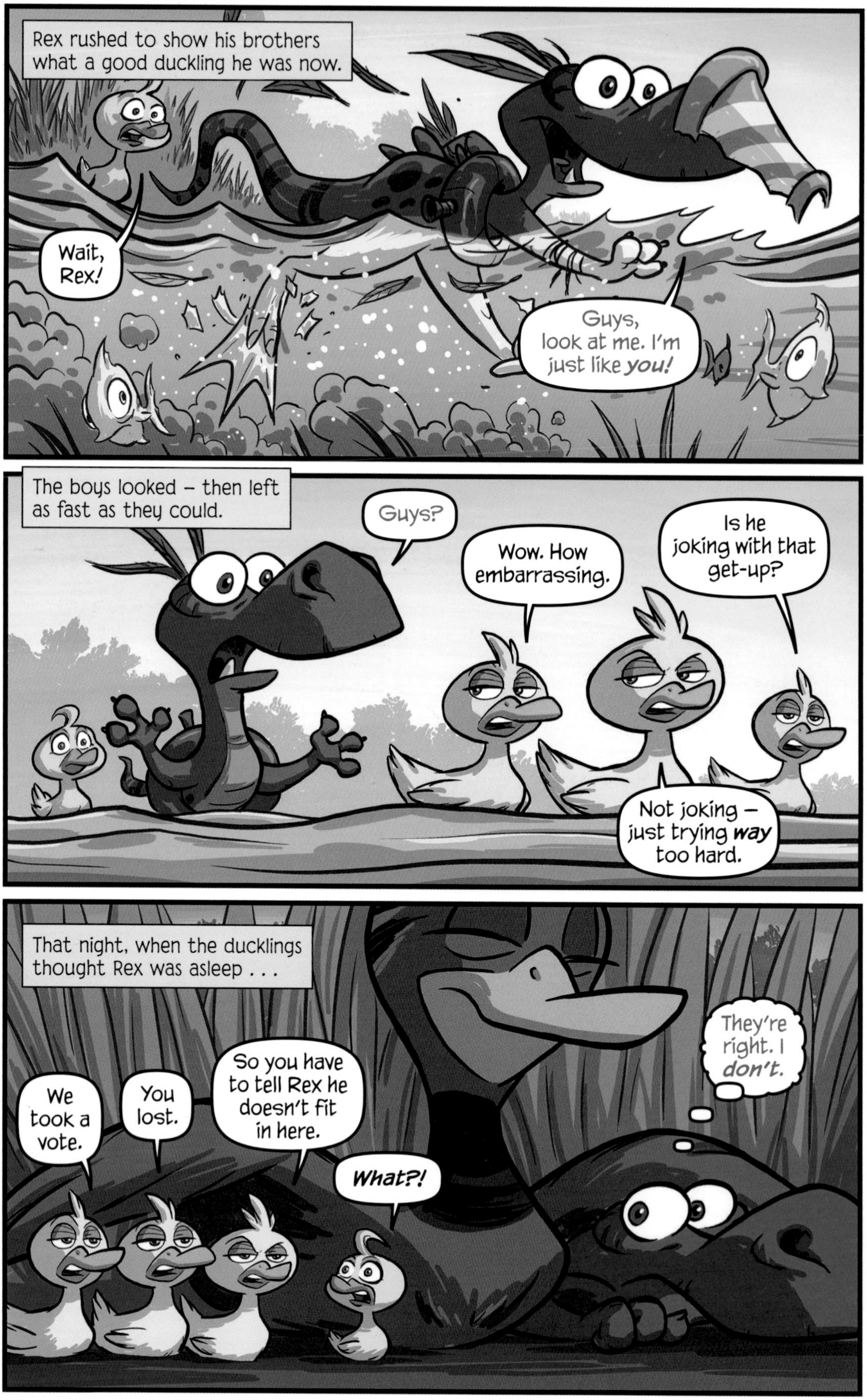
Rex rushed to show his brothers what a good duckling he was now.
Wait, Rex!
Guys, look at me. I'm just like *you!*
The boys looked – then left as fast as they could.
Guys?
Wow. How embarrassing.
Is he joking with that get-up?
Not joking – just trying *way* too hard.
That night, when the ducklings thought Rex was asleep . . .
We took a vote.
You lost.
So you have to tell Rex he doesn't fit in here.
What?!
They're right. I *don't.*

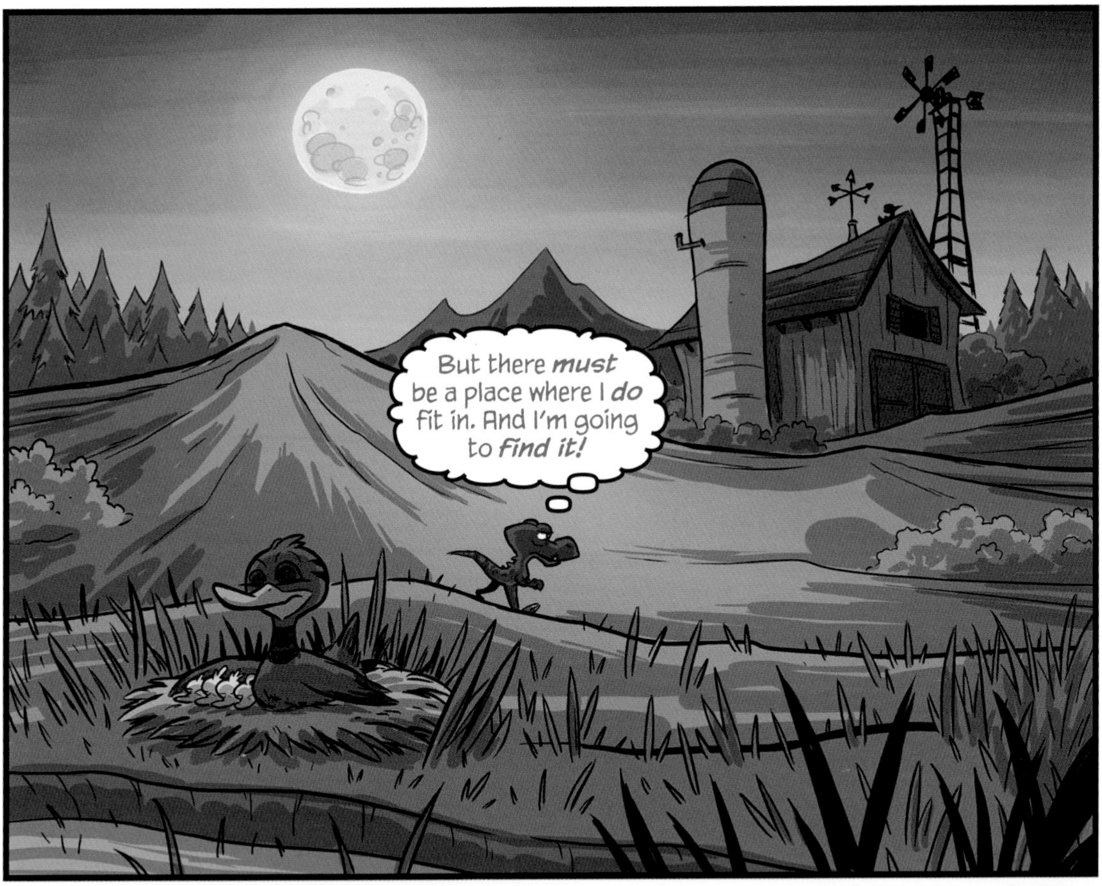
But there **must** be a place where I **do** fit in. And I'm going to **find it!**

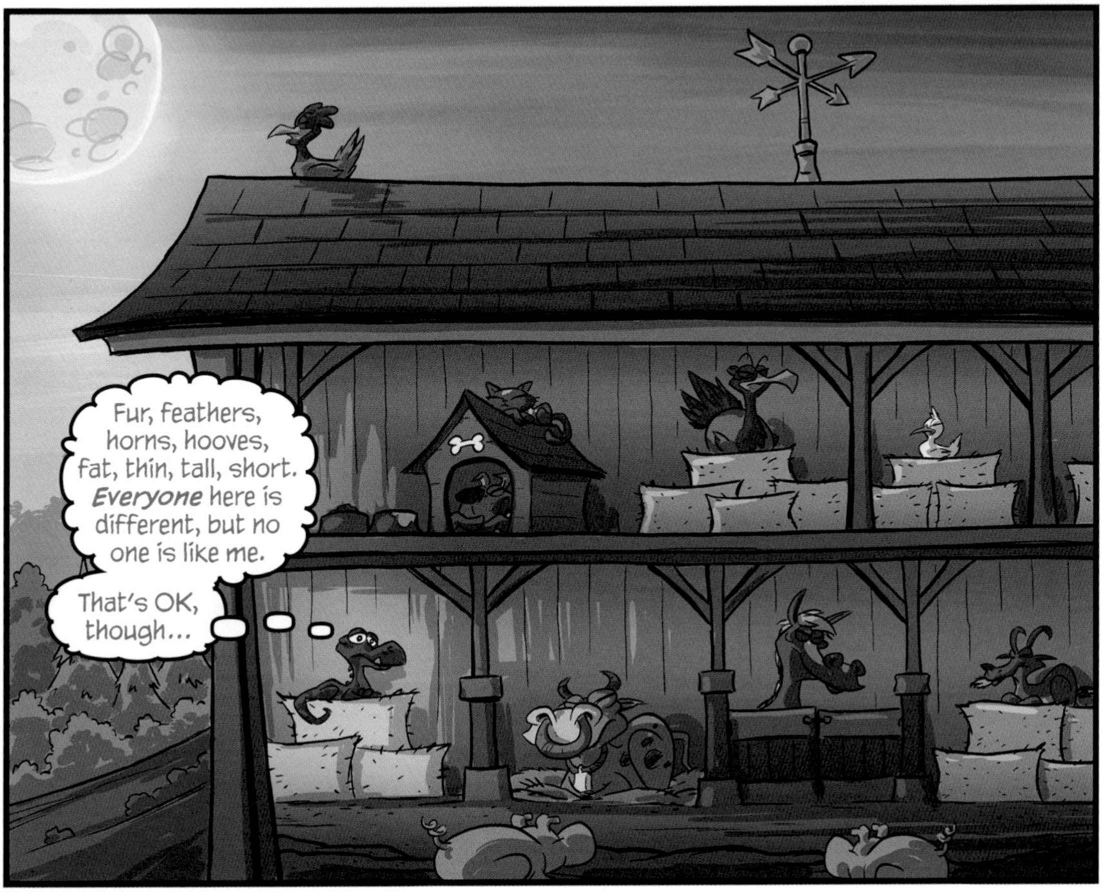
Fur, feathers, horns, hooves, fat, thin, tall, short. **Everyone** here is different, but no one is like me.
That's OK, though...

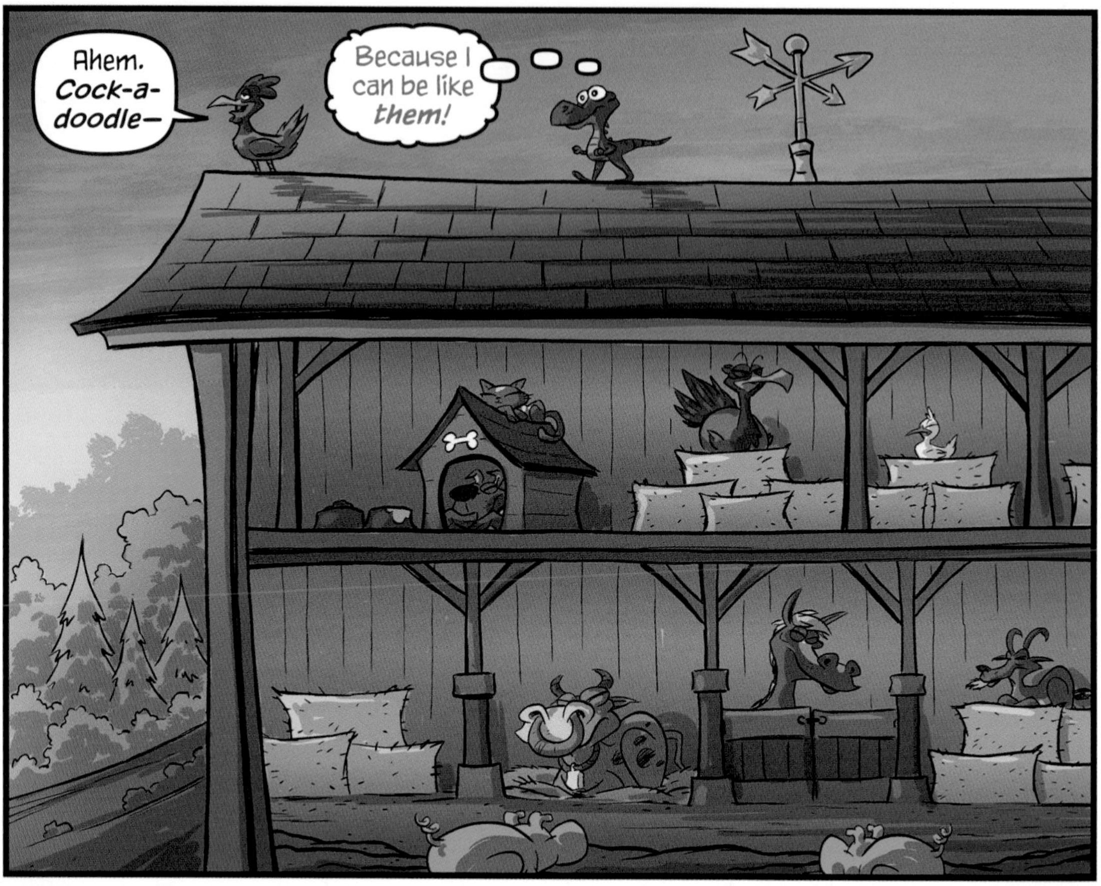
Ahem. *Cock-a-doodle—*
Because I can be like *them!*

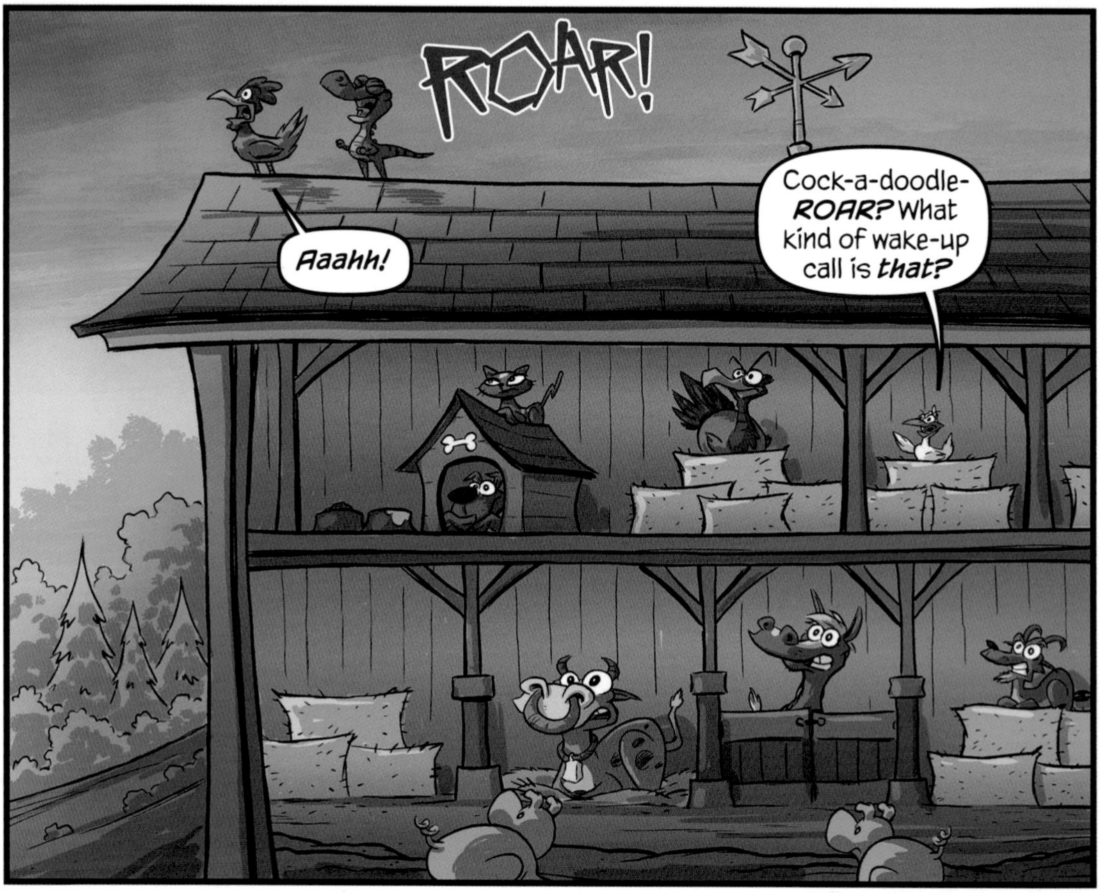
ROAR!
Aaahh!
Cock-a-doodle-*ROAR?* What kind of wake-up call is *that?*

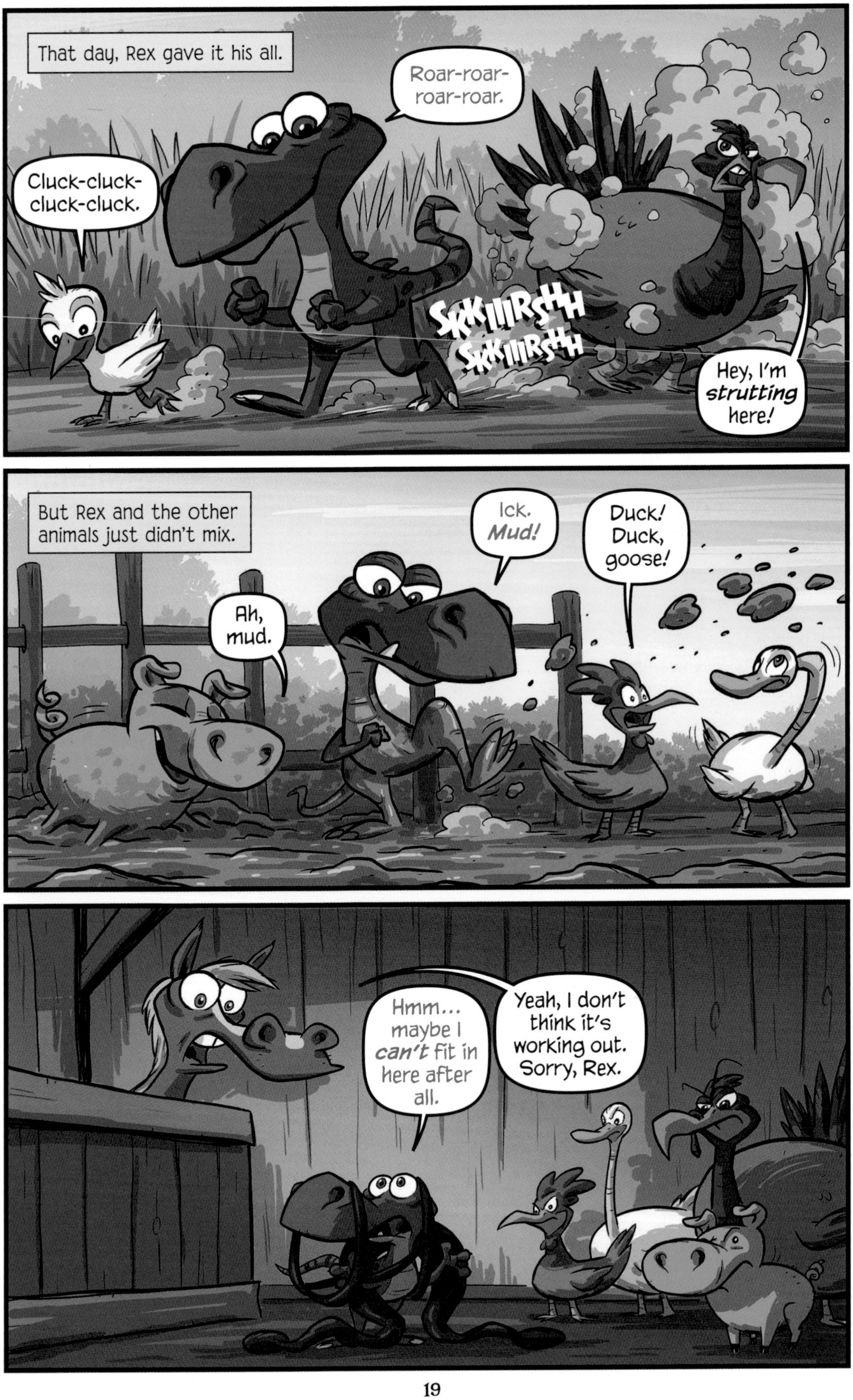
That day, Rex gave it his all.
Cluck-cluck-cluck-cluck.
Roar-roar-roar-roar.
SKKIIIRSHH SKKIIIRSHH
Hey, I'm *strutting* here!
But Rex and the other animals just didn't mix.
Ah, mud.
Ick. *Mud!*
Duck! Duck, goose!
Hmm... maybe I *can't* fit in here after all.
Yeah, I don't think it's working out. Sorry, Rex.

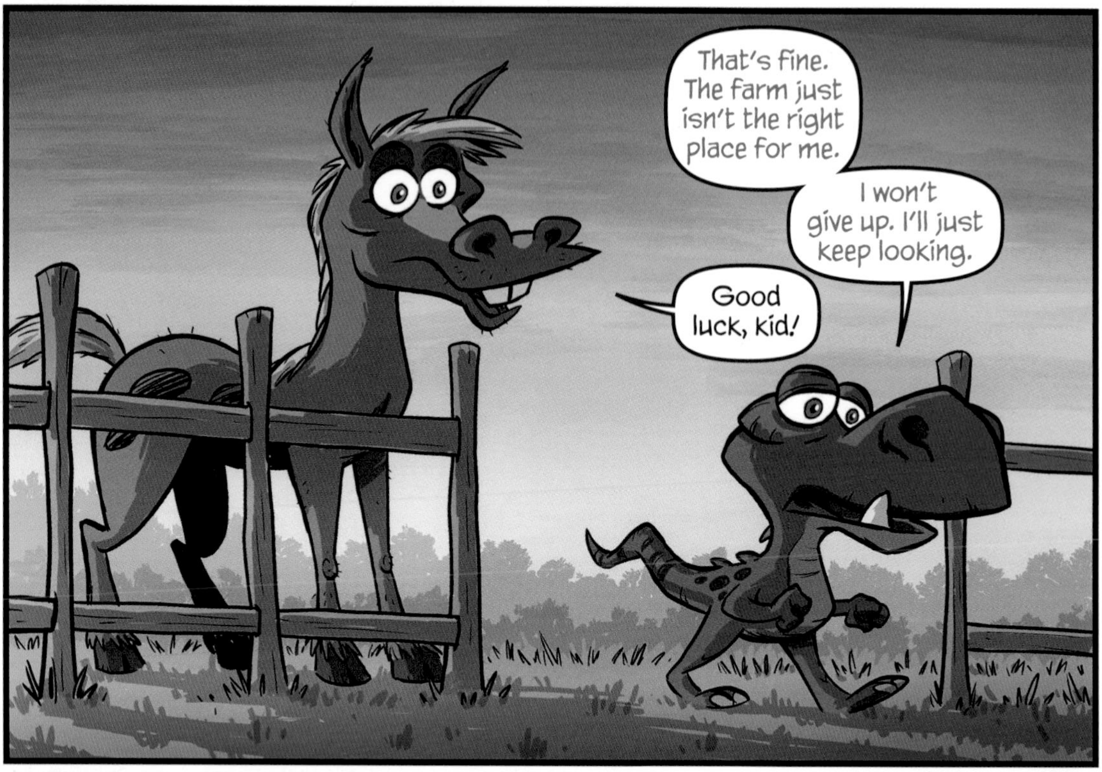
That's fine. The farm just isn't the right place for me.
I won't give up. I'll just keep looking.
Good luck, kid!

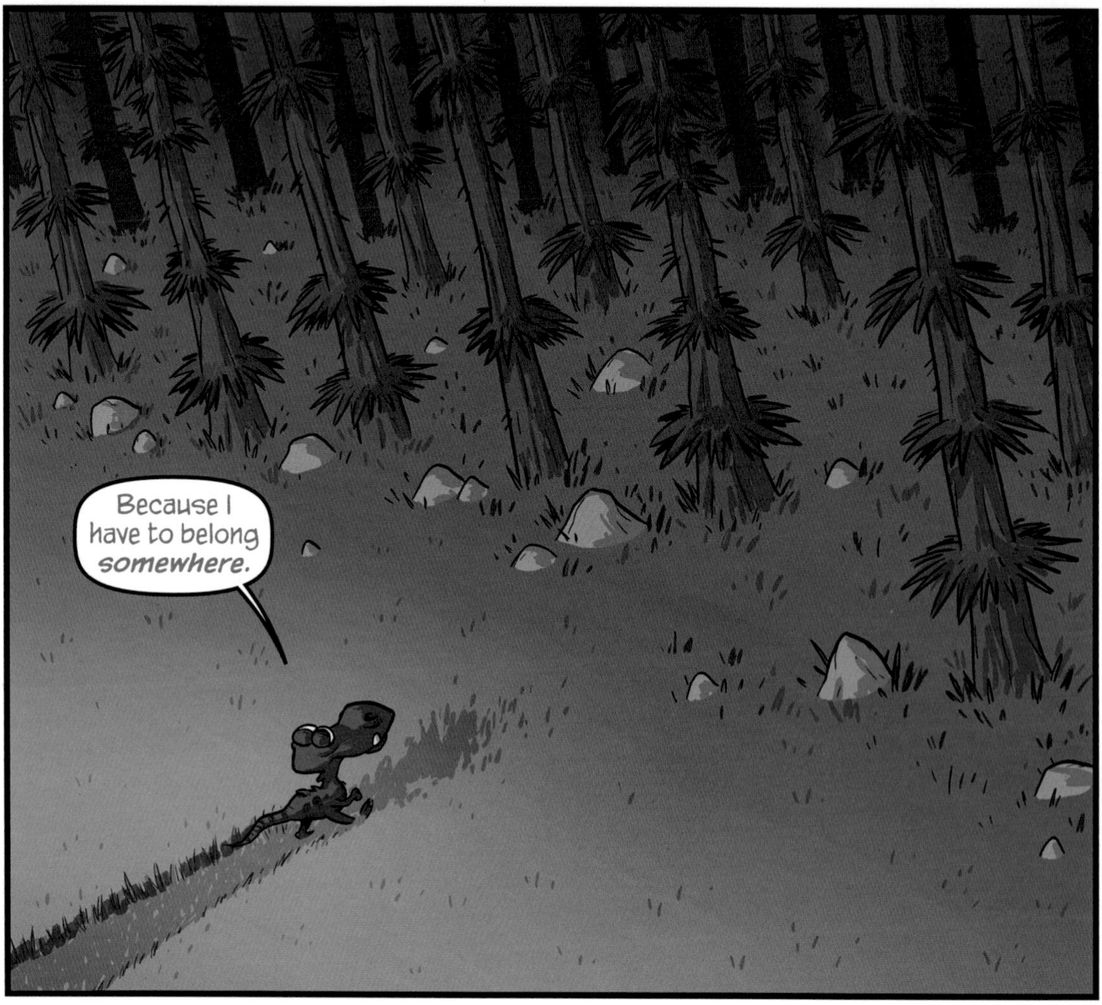
Because I have to belong *somewhere.*

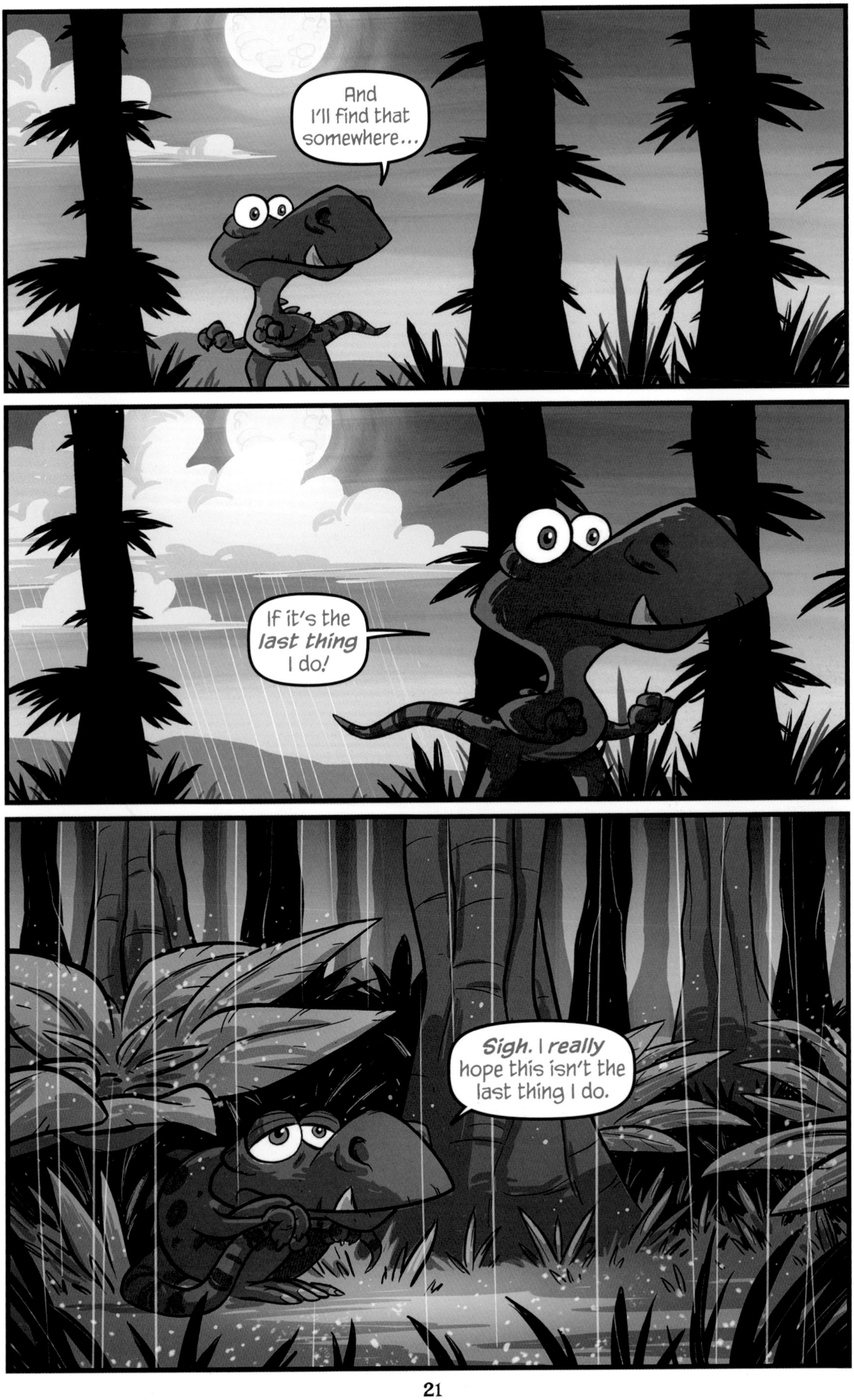
And I'll find that somewhere...
If it's the *last thing* I do!
Sigh. I *really* hope this isn't the last thing I do.

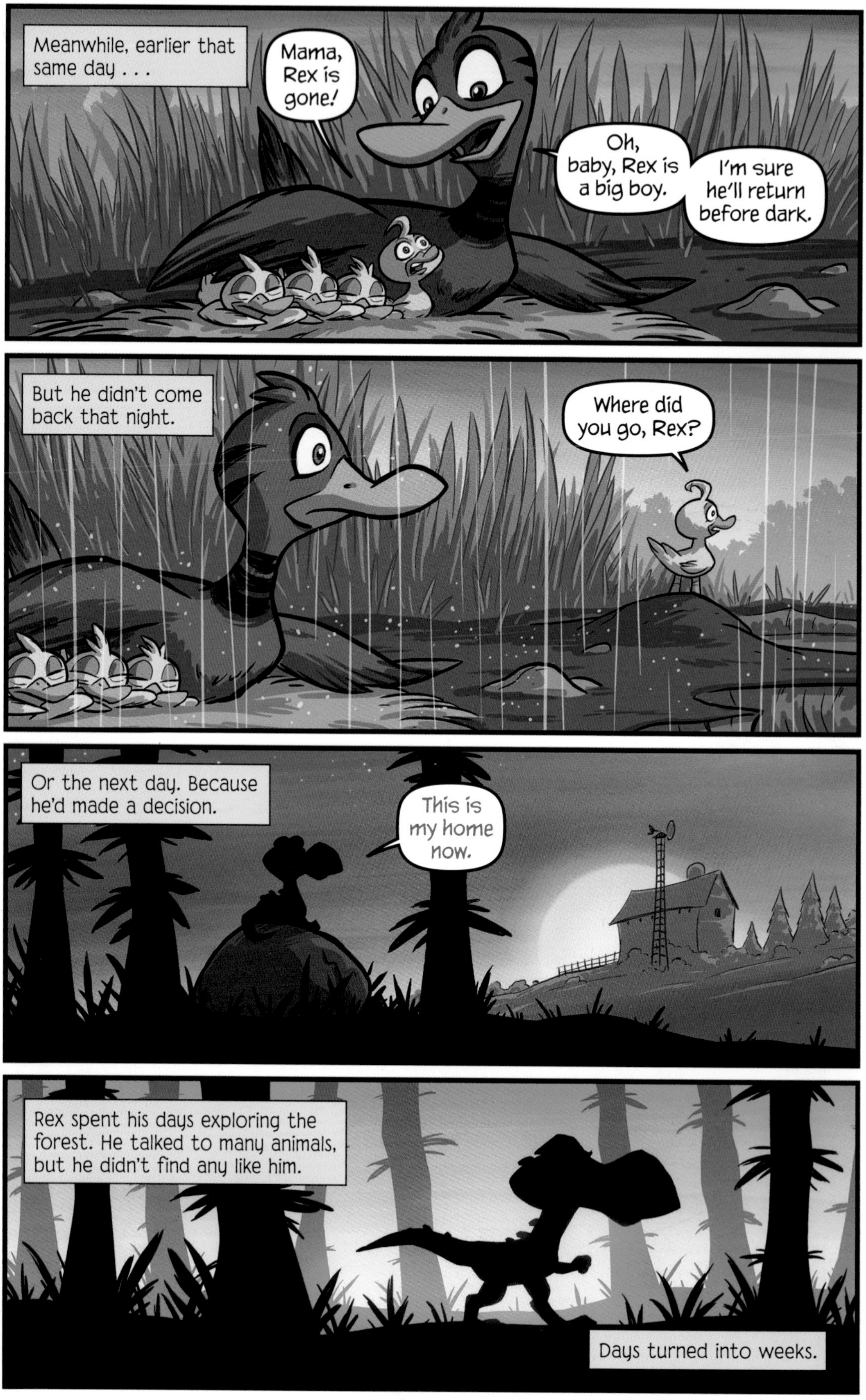

Meanwhile, earlier that same day . . .
Mama, Rex is gone!
Oh, baby, Rex is a big boy.
I'm sure he'll return before dark.
But he didn't come back that night.
Where did you go, Rex?
Or the next day. Because he'd made a decision.
This is my home now.
Rex spent his days exploring the forest. He talked to many animals, but he didn't find any like him.
Days turned into weeks.

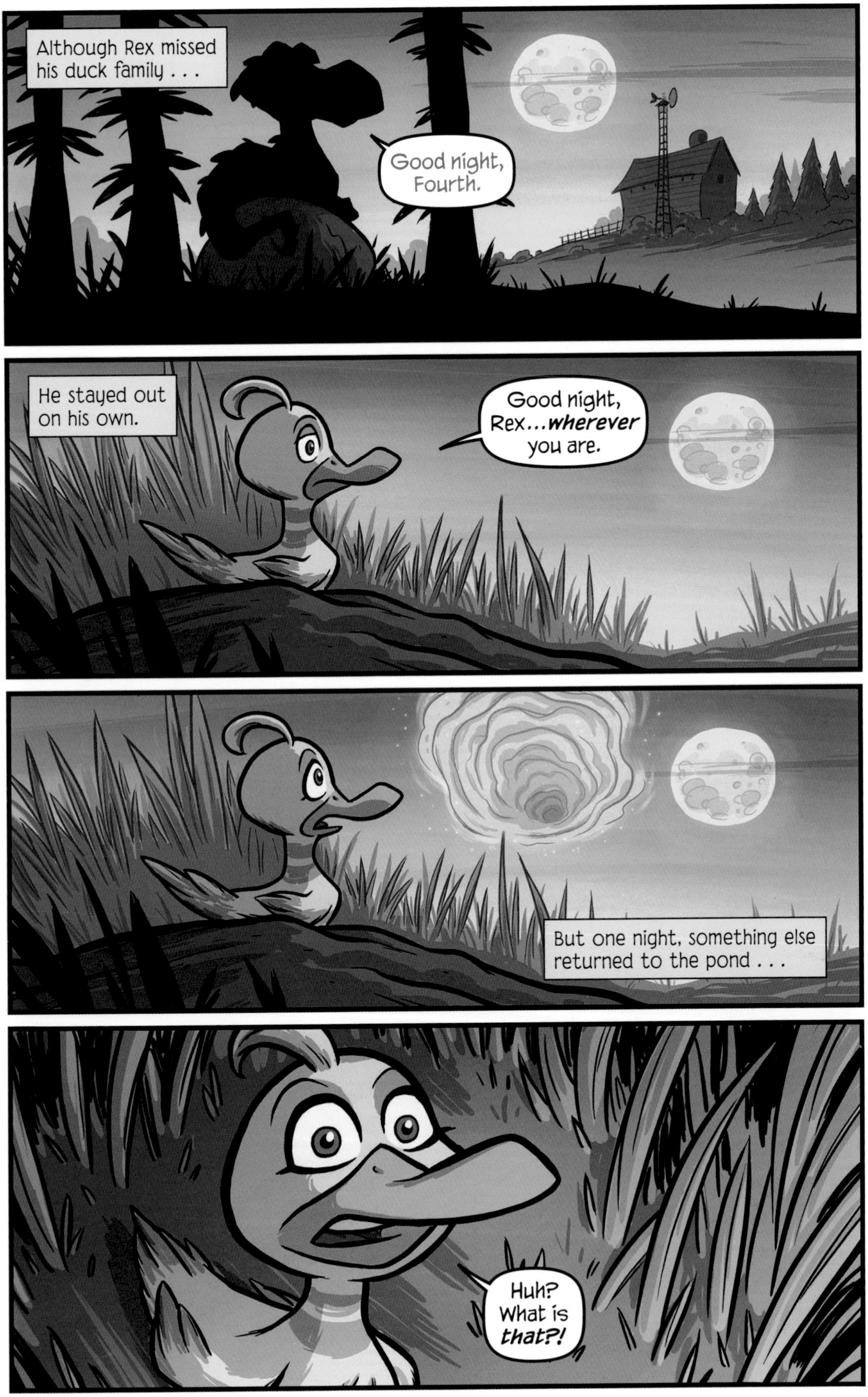
Although Rex missed his duck family . . .
Good night, Fourth.
He stayed out on his own.
Good night, Rex...*wherever* you are.
But one night, something else returned to the pond . . .
Huh? What is *that?!*

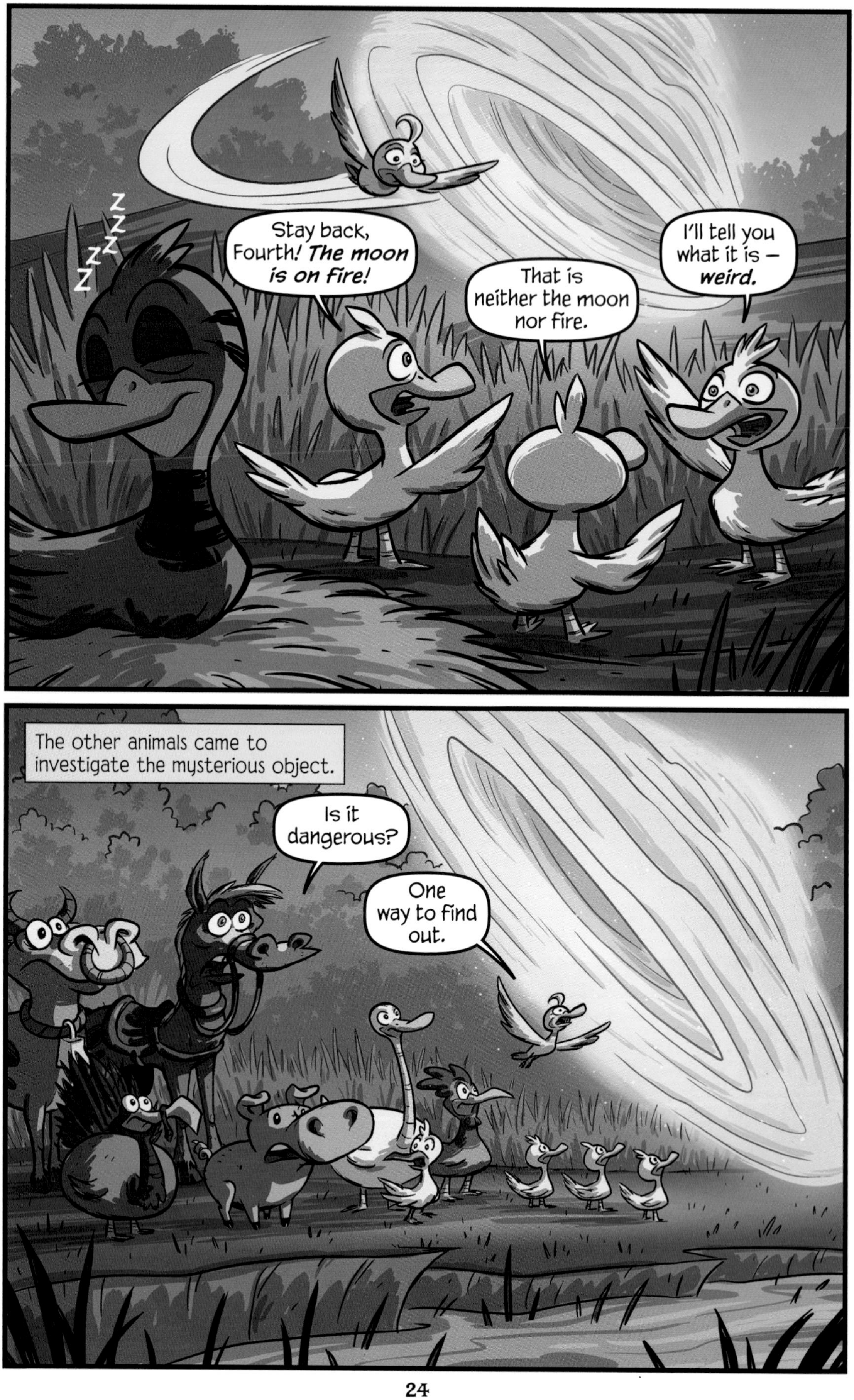
Z Z Z Z Z
Stay back, Fourth! *The moon is on fire!*
That is neither the moon nor fire.
I'll tell you what it is — ***weird.***
The other animals came to investigate the mysterious object.
Is it dangerous?
One way to find out.

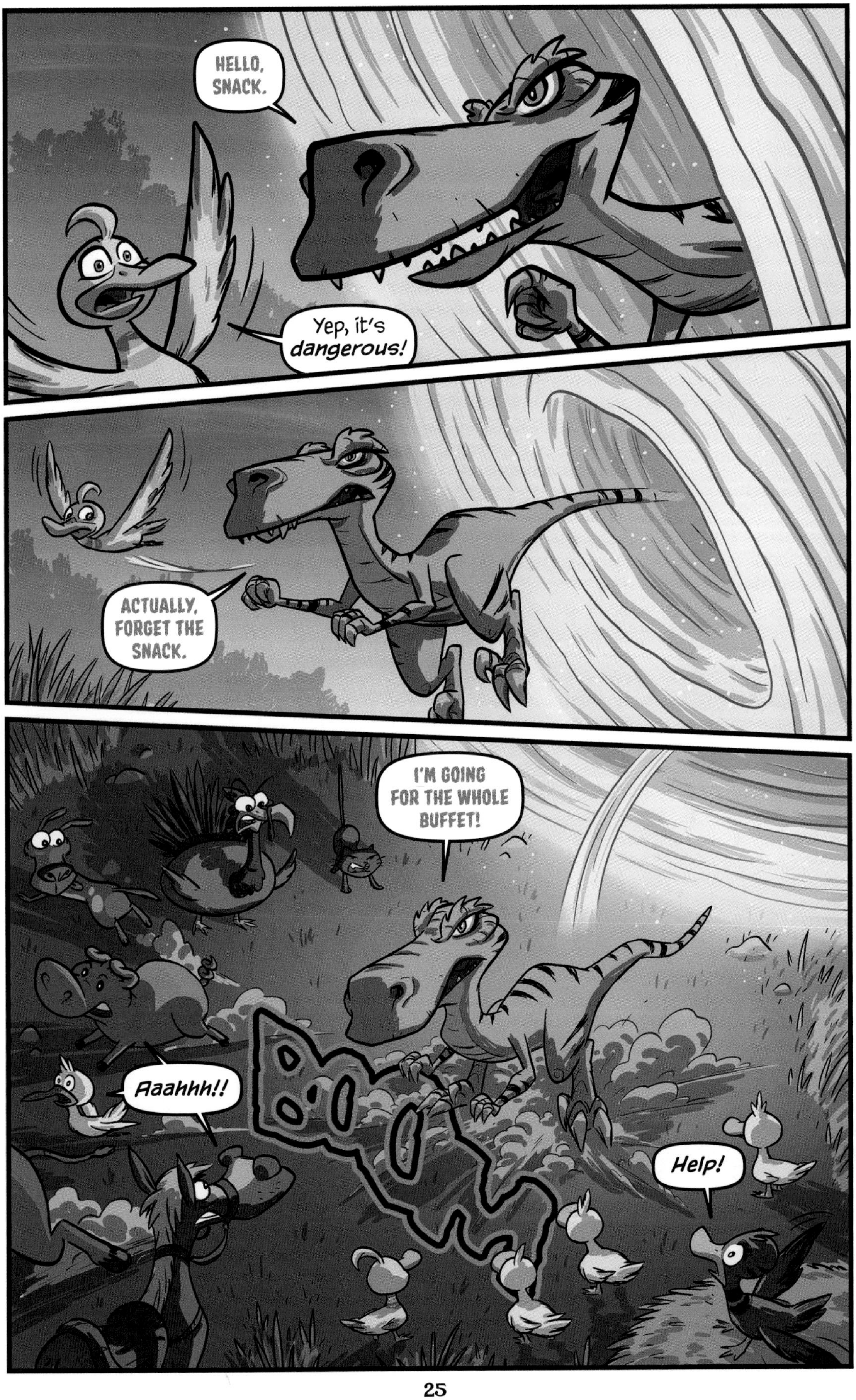
HELLO, SNACK.
Yep, it's *dangerous!*
ACTUALLY, FORGET THE SNACK.
I'M GOING FOR THE WHOLE BUFFET!
Aaahhh!!
Help!

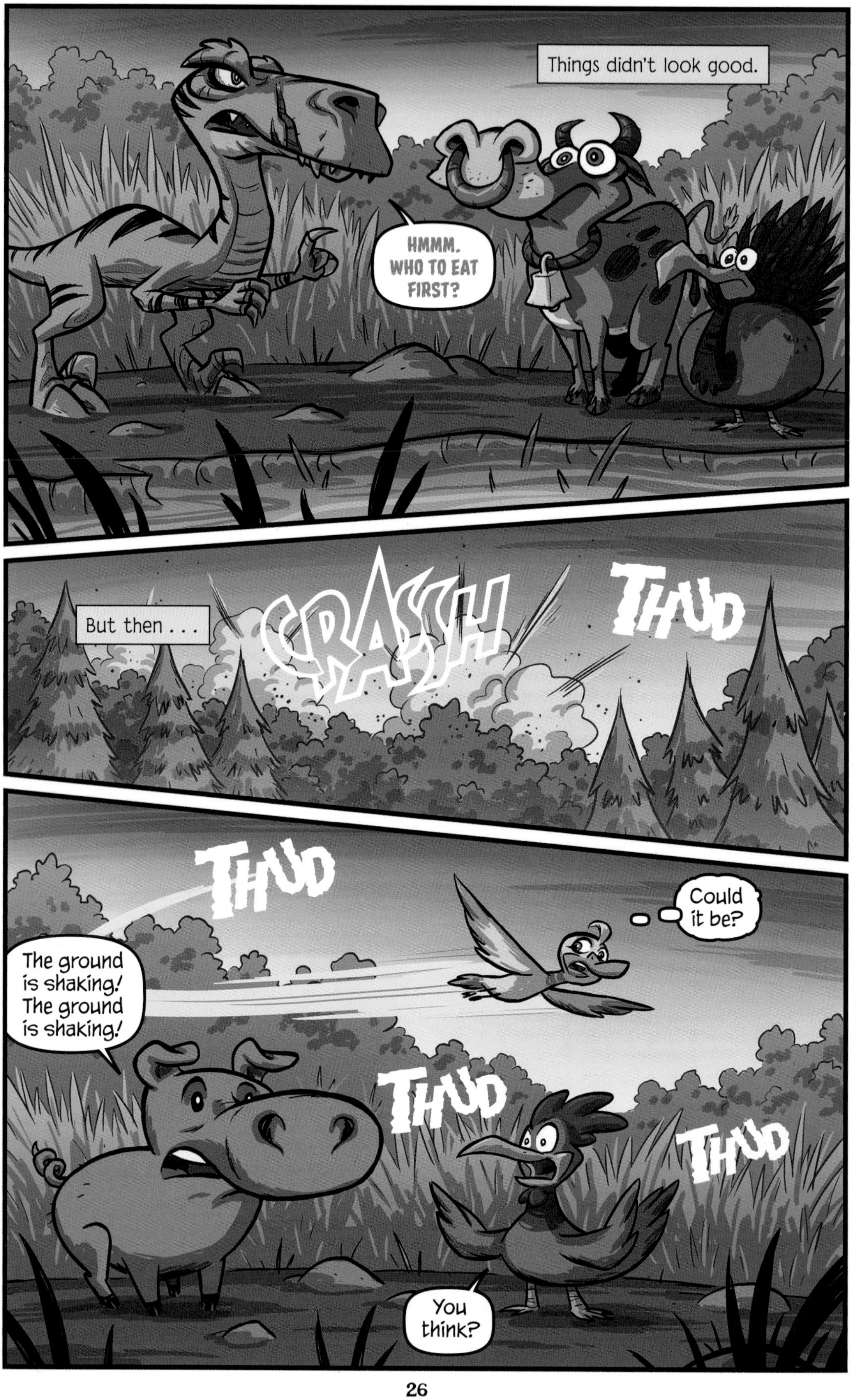
Things didn't look good.
HMMM. WHO TO EAT FIRST?
But then . . .
CRASH
THUD
THUD
Could it be?
The ground is shaking! The ground is shaking!
THUD
THUD
You think?

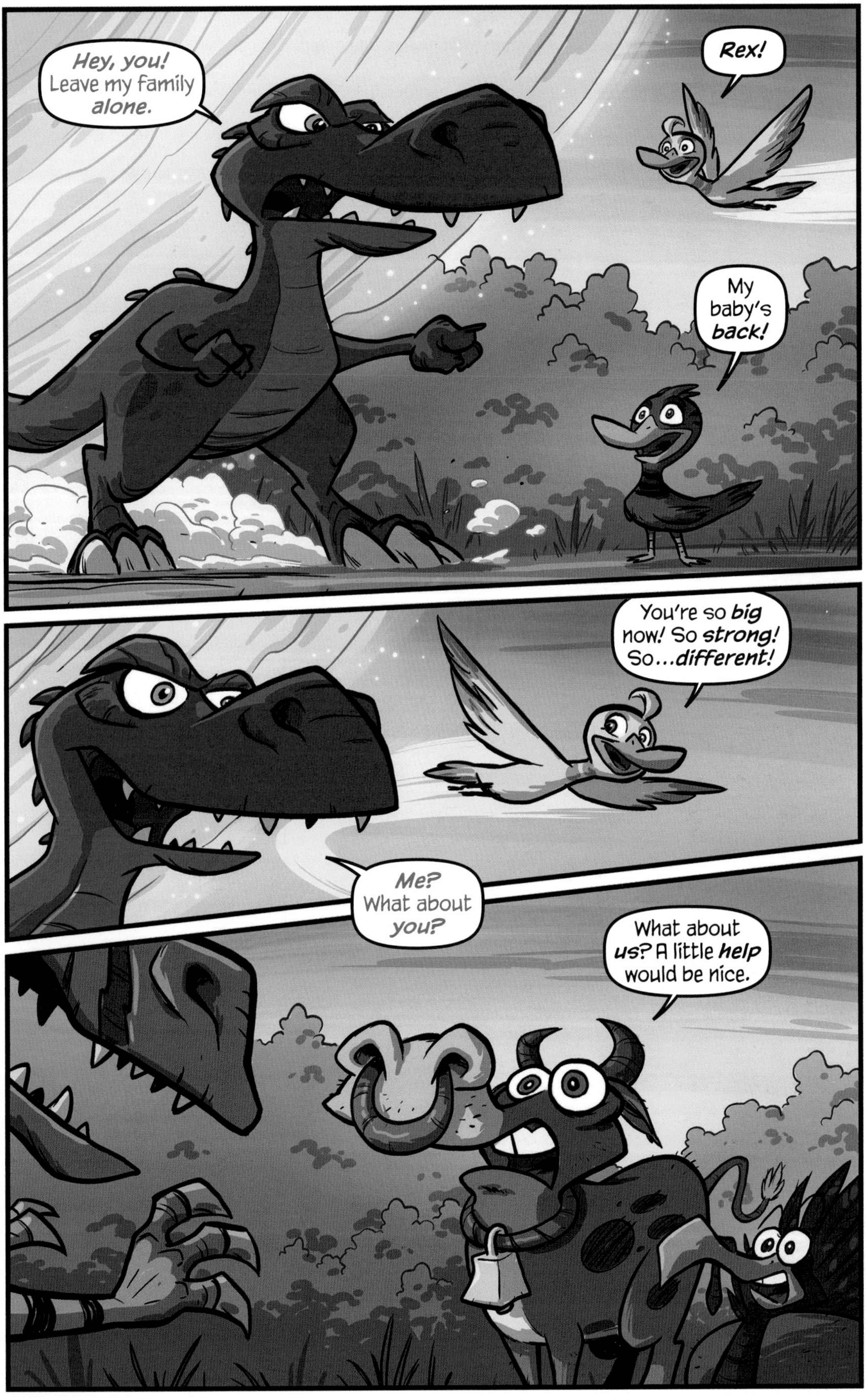
Hey, you! Leave my family alone.
Rex!
My baby's back!
You're so big now! So strong! So...different!
Me? What about you?
What about us? A little help would be nice.

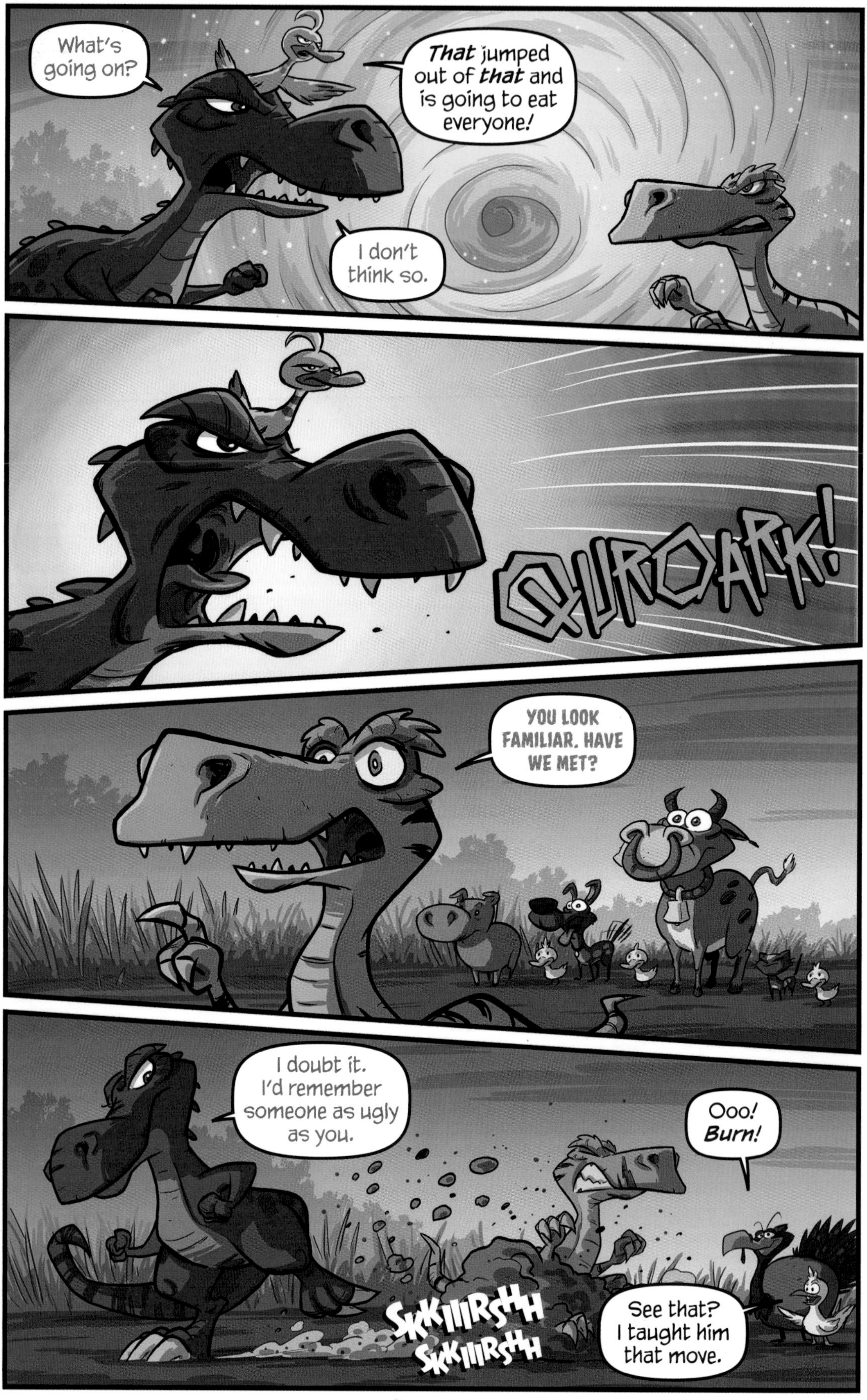

What's going on?
That jumped out of that and is going to eat everyone!
I don't think so.
QUROARK!
YOU LOOK FAMILIAR. HAVE WE MET?
I doubt it. I'd remember someone as ugly as you.
Ooo! Burn!
SKKIIIRSHH SKKIIIRSHH
See that? I taught him that move.

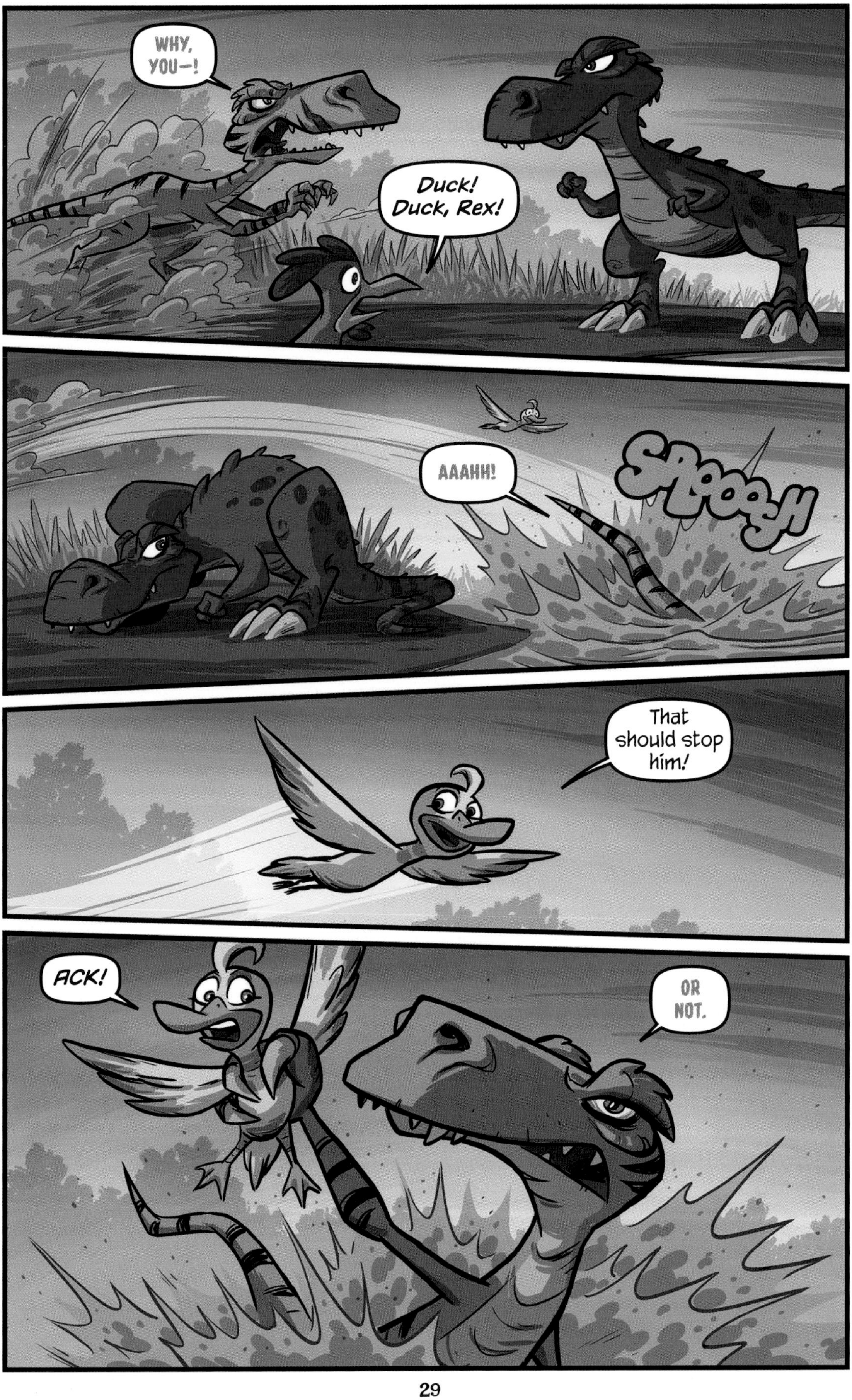
WHY, YOU—!
Duck! Duck, Rex!
AAAHH!
SPLOOOSH
That should stop him!
ACK!
OR NOT.

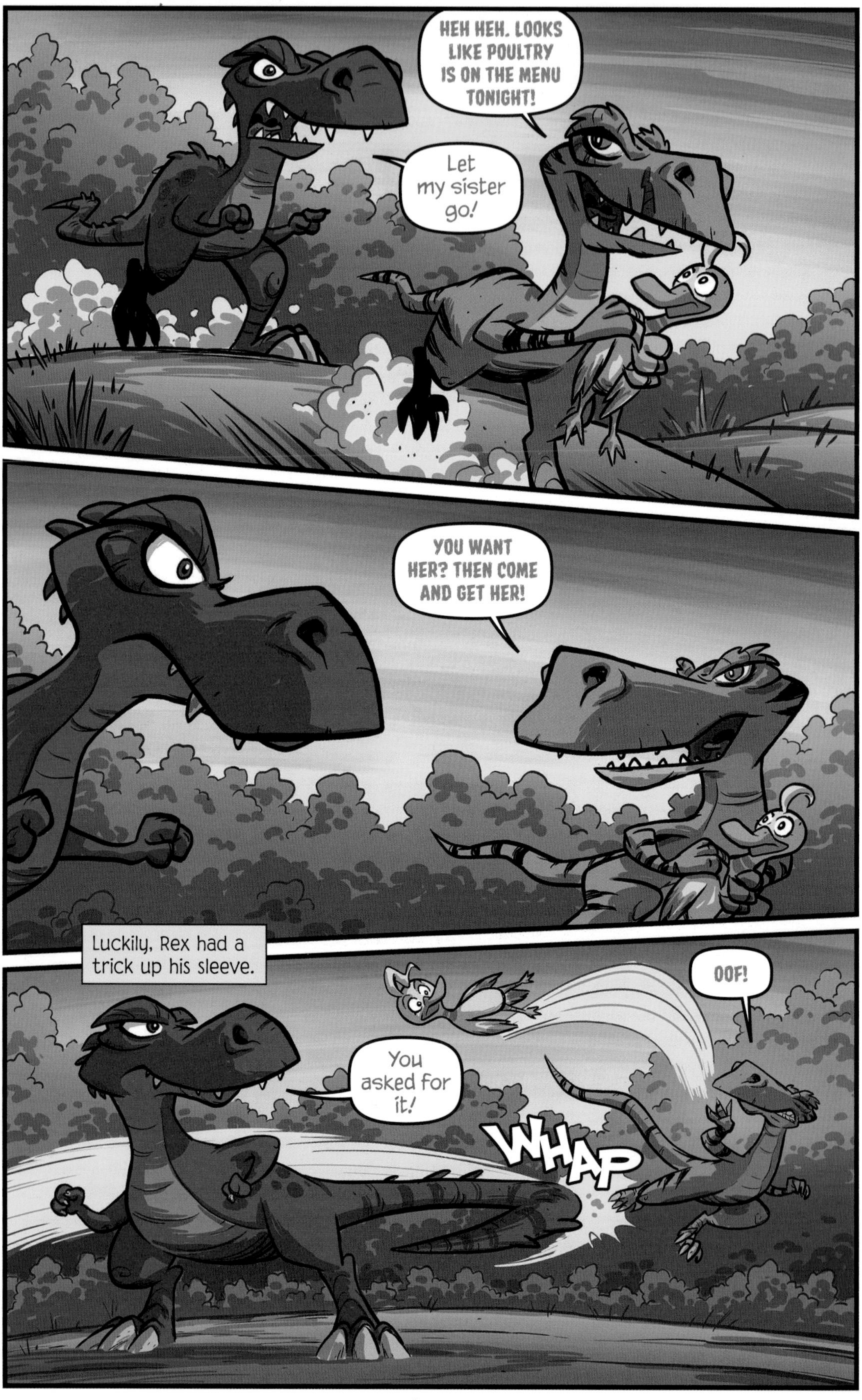
HEH HEH. LOOKS LIKE POULTRY IS ON THE MENU TONIGHT!
Let my sister go!
YOU WANT HER? THEN COME AND GET HER!
Luckily, Rex had a trick up his sleeve.
You asked for it!
OOF!
WHAP

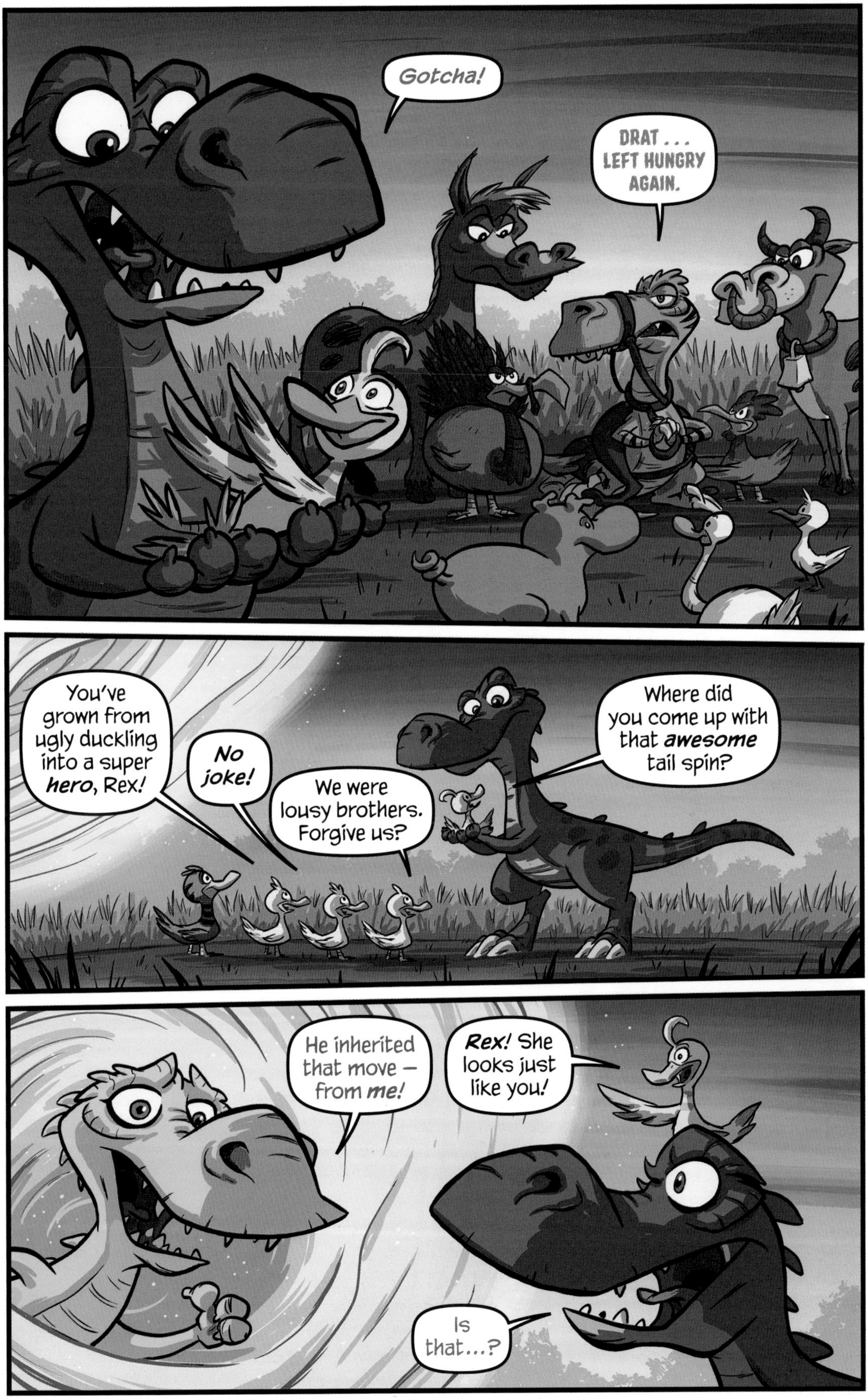

Gotcha!
DRAT . . . LEFT HUNGRY AGAIN.
You've grown from ugly duckling into a super **hero**, Rex!
No joke!
We were lousy brothers. Forgive us?
Where did you come up with that ***awesome*** tail spin?
He inherited that move — from ***me!***
Rex! She looks just like you!
Is that...?

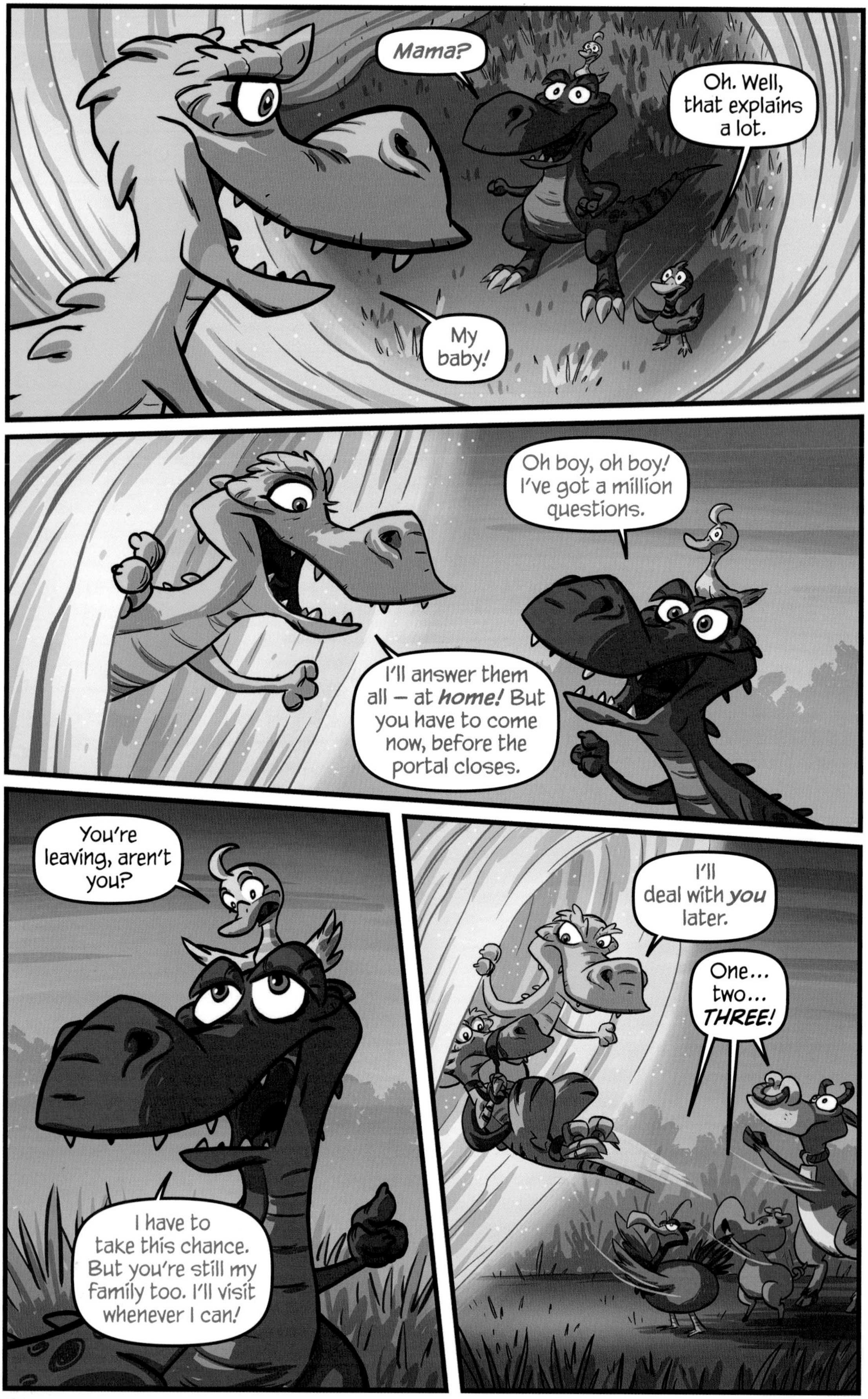
Mama?
Oh. Well, that explains a lot.
My baby!
Oh boy, oh boy! I've got a million questions.
I'll answer them all — at *home!* But you have to come now, before the portal closes.
You're leaving, aren't you?
I have to take this chance. But you're still my family too. I'll visit whenever I can!
I'll deal with *you* later.
One... two... *THREE!*

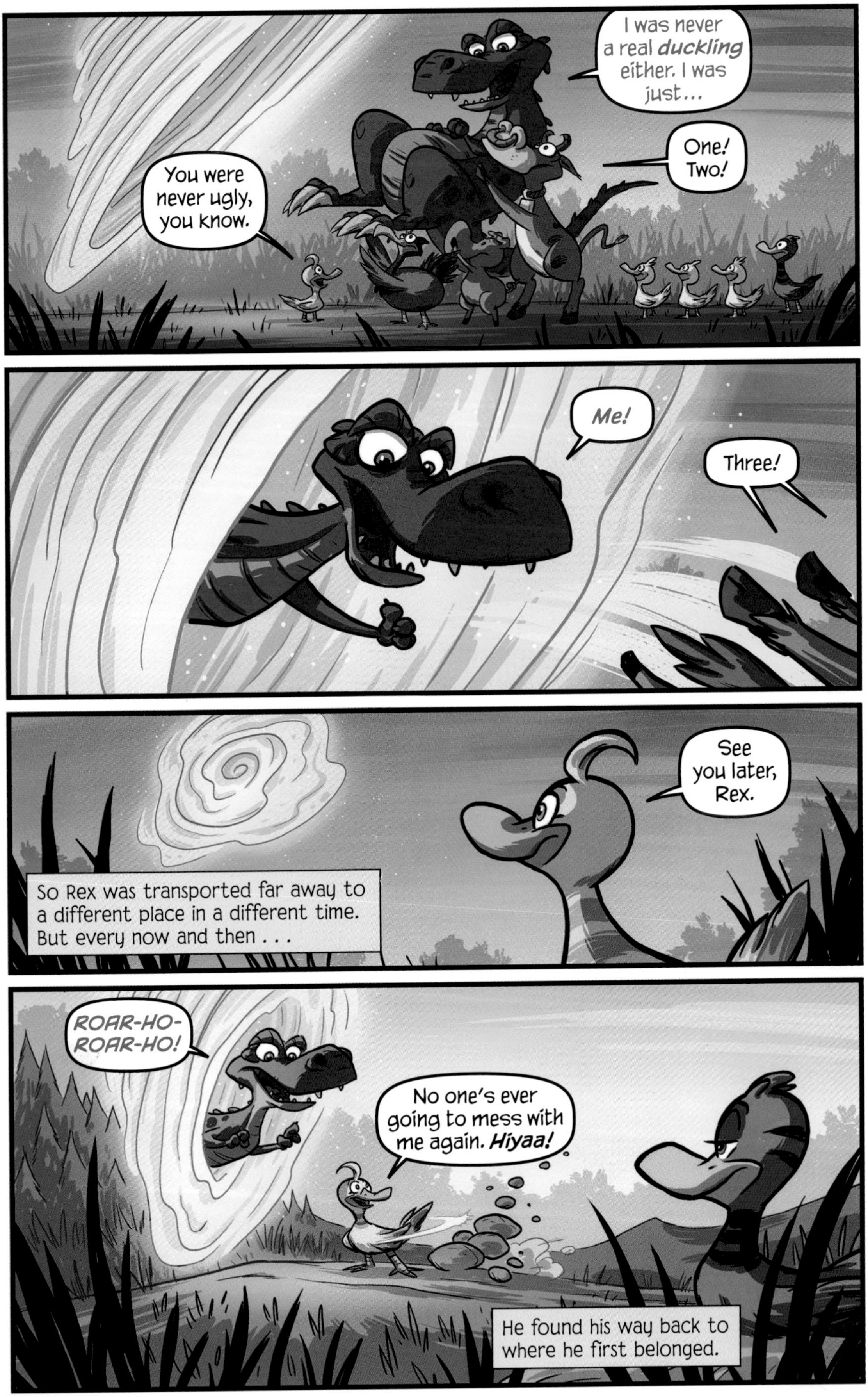
I was never a real *duckling* either. I was just...
You were never ugly, you know.
One! Two!
Me!
Three!
See you later, Rex.
So Rex was transported far away to a different place in a different time. But every now and then . . .
ROAR-HO-ROAR-HO!
No one's ever going to mess with me again. *Hiyaa!*
He found his way back to where he first belonged.

ALL ABOUT FABLES

A fable is a short tale that teaches the reader a lesson about life, often with animal characters. At the end of a fable, there's almost always a moral (a fancy word for lesson) stated right out so you don't miss it. Yeah, fables can be kind of bossy. But luckily, they usually give pretty good advice. Read on to learn more about the original fable written by Danish author Hans Christian Andersen in 1843, and its moral. Can you spot any other lessons?

THE UGLY DUCKLING

One day, a swan egg rolls into a duck's nest. When all the eggs hatch, the baby swan – called a cygnet – looks a lot different from the ducklings. Although the cygnet swims better than his siblings, the barnyard animals tease him and call him ugly. Soon, even the mother duck says he doesn't belong. So the baby swan decides to run away. He tries living with wild ducks and then with an old lady and her pets. But he doesn't fit in. Out on his own, the cygnet nearly freezes during winter. In spring, the cygnet spots a flock of majestic swans. He's afraid they'll pick on him like everyone else has. But to his astonishment, they greet him with respect. Because he isn't an ugly duckling anymore. He's grown into the most beautiful swan in the entire pond.

THE MORAL

NEVER GIVE UP ON FINDING WHERE YOU BELONG
(In other words, don't change who
you are to fit in – find
where you're valued
for being YOU!)

A **FAR OUT** GUIDE TO THE FABLE'S JURASSIC TWISTS!

The swan egg is swapped out for a dinosaur egg that has tumbled through a time portal!

In the original, even the duck mom and siblings teased the ugly duckling. Here, Fourth encourages Rex to stay true to himself.

The ugly duckling turns into a beautiful swan, but Rex grows up to use his awesome dino abilities to rescue the farm animals.

The swan leaves the ducks of the pond far behind. Rex still visits his duck family!

VISUAL QUESTIONS

The animals judge Rex because of how he looks. Do you think that's fair? Have you ever felt like you didn't fit in? Talk about your answers.

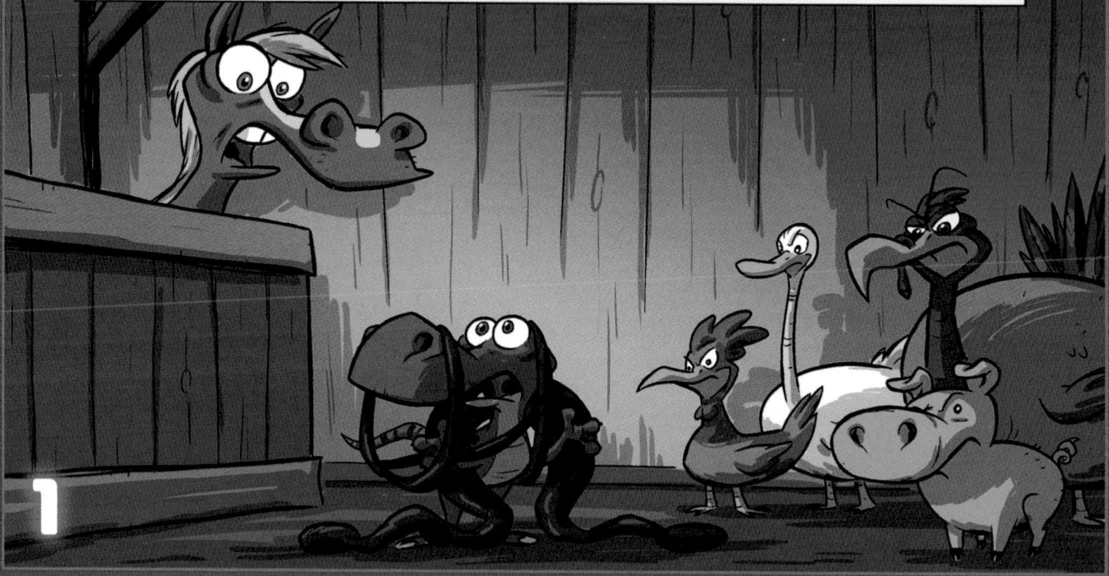
1

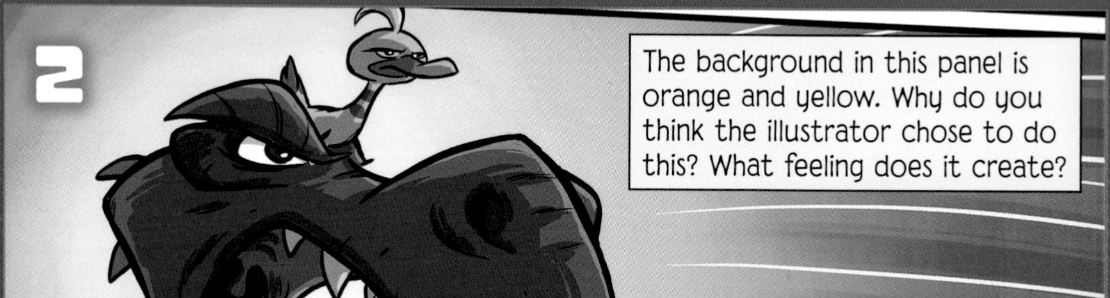
2

The background in this panel is orange and yellow. Why do you think the illustrator chose to do this? What feeling does it create?

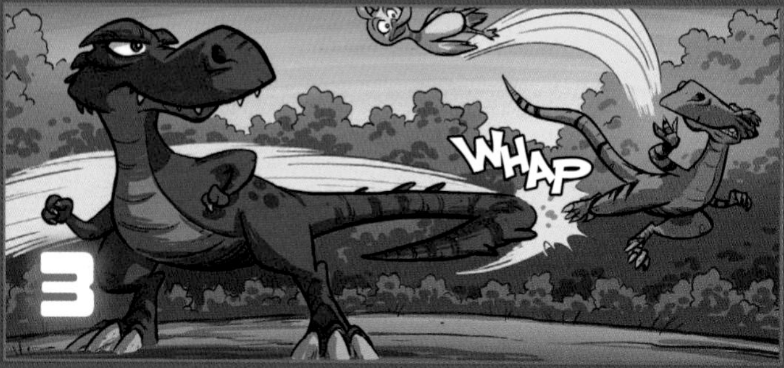
WHAP
3

Rex is teased for being different, but his differences help to save the day. In your own words, discuss how Rex uses his unique dinosaur abilities to defeat the velociraptor.

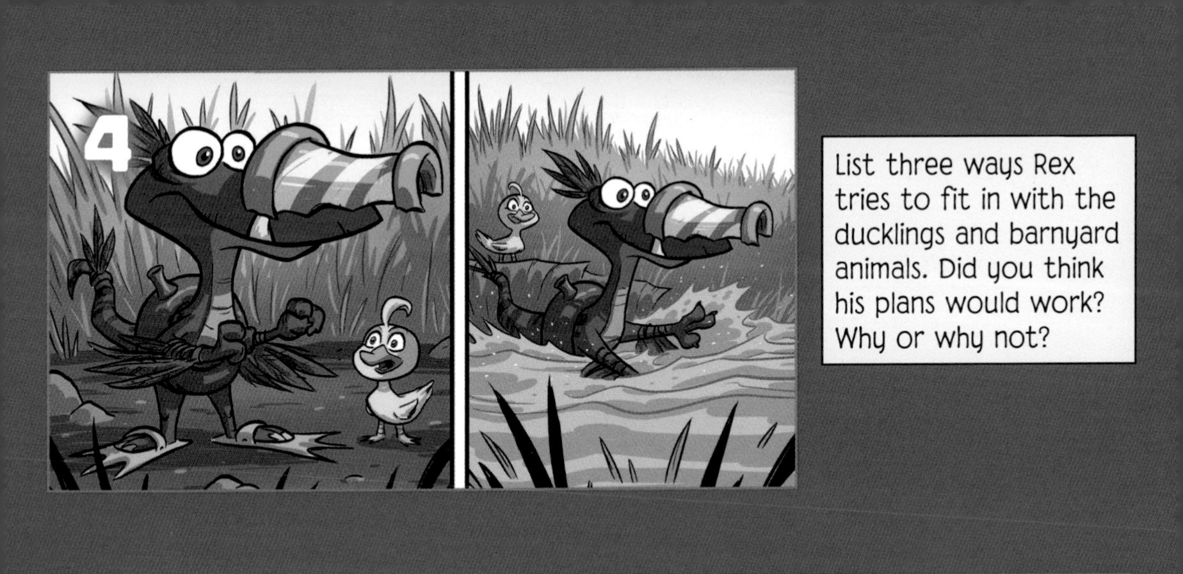

4

List three ways Rex tries to fit in with the ducklings and barnyard animals. Did you think his plans would work? Why or why not?

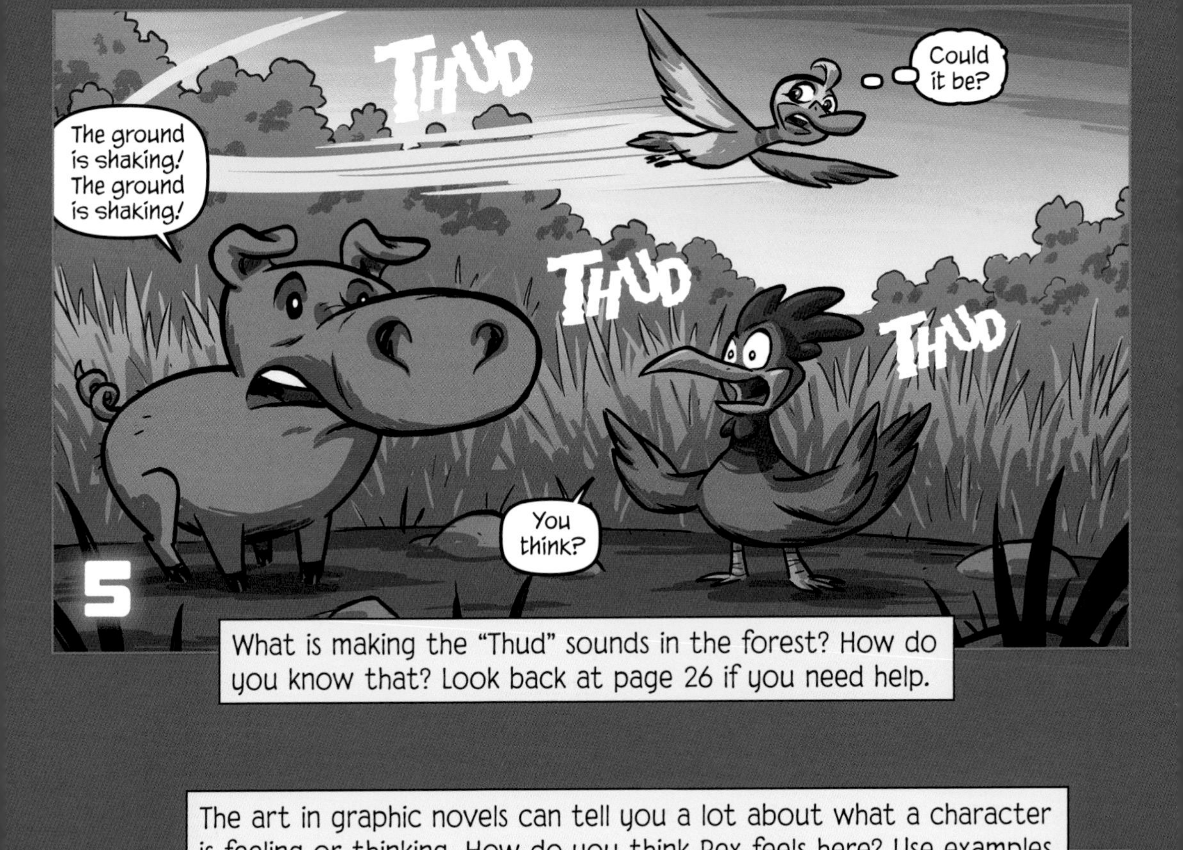
THUD
Could it be?
The ground is shaking! The ground is shaking!
THUD
THUD
You think?

5

What is making the “Thud” sounds in the forest? How do you know that? Look back at page 26 if you need help.

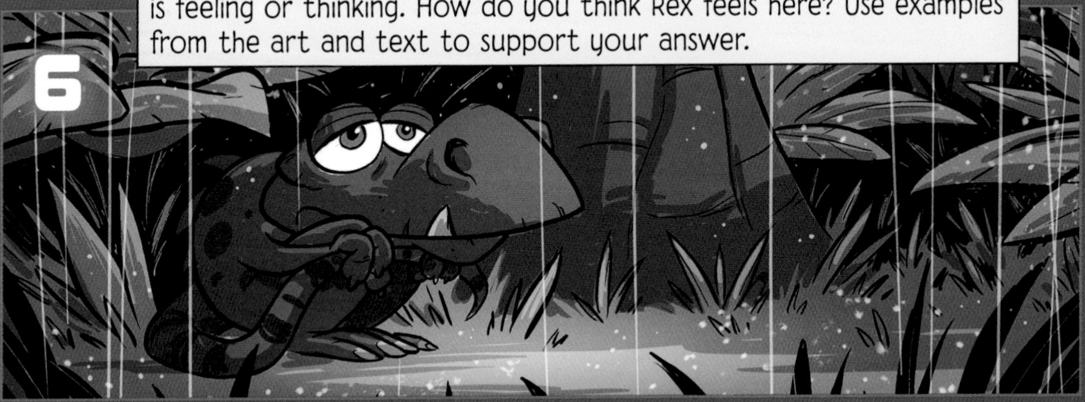

6

The art in graphic novels can tell you a lot about what a character is feeling or thinking. How do you think Rex feels here? Use examples from the art and text to support your answer.

AUTHOR

Stephanie Peters worked as a children's book editor for ten years before she started writing books herself. She has since written forty books, including *Sleeping Beauty*, *Magic Master* and the New York Times best-seller *A Princess Primer: A Fairy Godmother's Guide to Being a Princess*. When not at her computer, Peters enjoys playing with her two children, hitting the gym, or working on home improvement projects with her patient and supportive husband, Daniel.

ILLUSTRATOR

Otis Frampton is a writer and artist. He is the creator of *Oddly Normal*, published by Image Comics. He is also one of the artists on the popular animated web series *How It Should Have Ended*.

GLOSSARY

decision (di-SIZH-uhn)—the act of making up your mind on what to do

eon (EE-on)—a long period of time that can't be measured

explore (ik-SPLOR)—to travel through a new area in order to learn or for adventure

familiar (fuh-MIL-yer)—well known or easily recognized; if something *seems* familiar, you're not quite sure if you know it and can't fully remember

inherit (in-HER-it)—to receive something from a parent, such as looks, habits, or skills

insist (in-SIST)—to demand or ask in a very firm way

overlook (oh-ver-LOOK)—to ignore or not pay attention to something

portal (POHR-tuhl)—a large, impressive opening or entrance

poultry (POHL-tree)—birds raised for their eggs and meat; chickens, turkeys, ducks, and geese are poultry

precious (PRESH-uhs)—having great importance or value

strut (STRUHT)—to walk in a proud way

unique (yoo-NEEK)—one of a kind and unlike anything else

wreck (REK)—to destroy or damage in a violent way

THE MORAL OF THE STORY IS... EPIC!

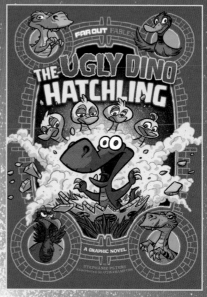

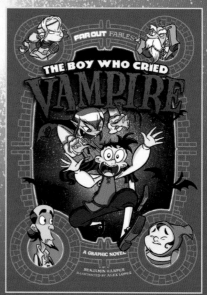

FAR OUT FABLES

ONLY FROM capstone